E. T. A. HOFFMANN

NUTCRACKER

ROBERTO INNOCENTI

Designed by Rita Marshall

CREATIVE EDITIONS

Mankato

HARCOURT BRACE & COMPANY

New York San Diego London

Christmas Eve

the Christmas Presents

Marie's Sweetheart

Wonderful Events

the Battle

the Invalid

Christmas Eve

On the twenty-fourth of December, the Stahlbaum children were absolutely forbidden to go into the small family

———◆•◆•◆———

parlor—much less into the grand formal parlor—at any time or for any reason. So, as the evening twilight fell, Fritz

❀

and Marie sat huddled together in a corner of a back room. A spooky feeling crept over them, for the room grew

———◆•◆•◆———

dark and, in accordance with the family Christmas tradition, no can-

dles were lit.

Fritz whispered to his little sister Marie, who had just turned

seven, that since early that morning, he'd been hearing rattling and

rustling sounds inside the forbidden parlors, as well as a distant ham-

mering. What's more, a short time earlier a dark little man had tiptoed

past them with a big box under his arm.

Of course, Fritz reassured her, this little man was none other

than Godfather Drosselmeier.

At this news, Marie clapped her hands gleefully and cried,

"Oh! What pretty things do you think that Godfather has made for us

this time?"

Godfather Drosselmeier was anything but nice-looking. He was small and thin, with a sea of wrinkles on his face. A big black patch covered his right eye and there was not a single hair left on his whole head—which was why he always wore a wig made of finely spun white glass. This wig, which he had fashioned himself, was a real work of art.

Despite his appearance, Godfather Drosselmeier was an extremely clever man. He was fascinated by time, and so had learned everything there was to know about clocks and watches. Whenever one of the Stahlbaums' fancy clocks broke down and couldn't chime, Godfather Drosselmeier would come, take off his glass wig and his little yellow coat, put on a blue apron, and proceed to stick sharp-pointed instruments into the belly of the clock. His probing surgical manner was difficult to watch—especially for little Marie. But Godfather didn't really hurt the poor clock. On the contrary, it would soon come to life again and begin to whir and chime and strike as strong as ever, which made the entire family happy.

Whenever he visited, Godfather Drosselmeier always had something delightful hidden away in his pockets for the children. It might be a funny little man who would roll his eyes and bow, or a box out of which a bird would spring, or some other delightful toy. But for Christmas, he always created some special marvel, something that cost him infinite pains and labor to make. This explains why, once the special gift had been presented, the children's parents always took it away and put it carefully aside.

Fritz thought that, this Christmas, their present ought to be a huge castle through which great numbers of finely uniformed soldiers could drill and march. There would also be a second army that would come to storm the walls. The soldiers within would begin firing their cannons, until the entire castle was banging and thundering like mad.

"No, Fritz!" Marie interrupted. "No, Godfather Drosselmeier told me just recently about a beautiful garden. In this garden there is an enormous lake, and on this lake swans with gold collars swim and sing lovely music. A little girl comes through the garden to the lake whenever she likes, and she calls the swans and feeds them marzipan."

"Swans don't eat marzipan," Fritz pointed out rather rudely. "And not even Godfather Drosselmeier can make an entire garden. Anyway, whatever he brings us for Christmas is always taken away. That is why I like the toys Father and Mother give us much better. Those toys are for us to keep and we can play with them."

To keep up their spirits, the children continued to guess what Christmas presents might be coming their way. Marie reminded Fritz that Miss Gertrude, her big doll, was not doing very well these days. Scolding her was no use: Miss Gertrude was growing clumsy, tumbling to the floor every two or three minutes. As a result, her once pretty face had been scratched and her elegant clothes had grown worn. Marie also remembered the way Mama had smiled when Marie had said how much she admired her friend Gretchen's little parasol. Surely that smile meant a fine present to come. Fritz interrupted her to point out that what his stable needed was a red and wily fox, and that his army still lacked cavalry, as Papa was well aware.

However, both children were certain of one thing—their parents had gotten all sorts of wonderful toys for them. Indeed, at this very moment, Mama and Papa were laying out their presents in the parlor. Both Fritz and Marie also remembered that at Christmas time the Christ Child always tried to answer their wishes.

Marie fell into a thoughtful silence, but Fritz murmured to himself: "Yes, I'd really like a fox and some soldiers!"

It was now quite dark. Fritz and Marie sat closer together. It was as if soft invisible wings were fluttering around them, while a distant but unspeakably lovely strain of music was floating to their

ears. A gleam of light flashed across the wall. At once they knew that

the Christ Child had sped away on his shining wings to visit other

children.

Just then a bell tinkled–*Kling-ling! Kling-ling!* The parlor

doors flew open, and such brilliant light came pouring over them that

the children were frozen and could only gasp, "Oh! Oh!"

Father and Mother took them by the hands and said, "Come

now, darlings, and see what the Christ Child has brought for you."

———◆◆◆◆◆———

the Christmas Presents

I ask you, dear reader—Theodore, Anna, or Fritz, whatever your name may be—I ask you to conjure up a picture of the

Christmas tree in your own home spreading its sparkling, decorated branches over the delightful

presents beneath it. That will give you some idea of how these two children felt as they stood there speechless, their

eyes fixed on all the beautiful things.

These children certainly must have been very, very good throughout the year to be rewarded like this, for never before had they been treated to so many wonderful things. The big Christmas tree bore a crop of silver and gold apples, and its branches were heavy with buds and blossoms as well, in the form of sugared almonds, multicolored candies, and all sorts of other treats. Perhaps the prettiest aspect about this amazing tree, however, was that in the shadows of its branches hundreds of little tapers glittered like stars, inviting the children to pluck the flowers and fruit.

All around the tree, a breathtaking display of gifts shone and sparkled. Who could possibly describe them all?

Marie gazed speechless at a bevy of elegant dolls with every imaginable accessory available for them. Still better, a little silk dress with many-tinted ribbons was hung upon a projecting branch, so it could be admired from all sides. "Oh! what a lovely—what a darling dress!" Marie cried out. "Am I really going to be allowed to wear it?" To her, it was the most beautiful gift of all.

In the meantime, Fritz had found the coveted fox and put it through its paces a few times around the tabletop. He said that it seemed a tad wild, but that he was sure he would soon have it tamed. Then he got to work mustering his new squadron of soldiers, who were admirably outfitted with red-and-gold uniforms and real silver swords. They were all mounted on shining white horses that seemed made of pure silver as well.

When Marie and Fritz had calmed down a bit, they began to look through their new picture books, which were spread open so as to tempt them with the colorful pictures. These portrayed bright flowers, peoples from around the world, and of course children playing every sort of game. All of these children were painted so naturally that they looked alive and ready to speak.

Soon there came another tinkling of a bell. This announced the display of Godfather Drosselmeier's Christmas present, which had been set up on a table against the wall that was concealed by a curtain. When this curtain was pulled away, the children couldn't believe their eyes.

On a green lawn, bright with flowers, stood a magnificent castle with many shining windows and golden towers. Inside the castle, bells were chiming a tune. When the doors and windows swung open, you could see small but graceful ladies and gentlemen, wearing plumed hats and long robes down to their heels, walking up and down in all the rooms. The central hall blazed with the light from myriad little candles burning in the silver chandeliers. There were children in short doublets dancing to the music of the bells. A lord in an emerald green mantle came to a window, gestured, and then disappeared inside again. Even Godfather Drosselmeier himself—no taller than Papa's thumb—came now and again to stand at the castle door, then went back inside.

Fritz, leaning his arms on the table, stared at the beautiful castle and its residents. "Godfather Drosselmeier," he said, "let me go into your castle for a little while!"

"That can't possibly be done," answered Godfather Drosselmeier. He was right, of course. It was silly of Fritz to want to go into a castle that wasn't as tall as he was. Even Fritz had to admit that.

The ladies and gentlemen kept walking, the children kept dancing, the emerald lord kept looking out the window, and Godfather

Drosselmeier kept coming to the door, all in the same way as before.

After a little while Fritz cried impatiently, "Godfather Drosselmeier,

please come to another door!"

"That can't be done, my dear Fritz," answered Drosselmeier.

"Well then," Fritz said, "that green man who looks out so

often~make him walk around with the others."

"That can't be done either," Drosselmeier replied.

"Make the children come down, then," said Fritz. "I want to see

them up closer."

"*Nothing* like that can be done!" Drosselmeier cried impa~

tiently. "The machinery must work as it's doing now. It can't be

changed."

"Oh," said Fritz, slowly and coolly. "You say it can't be done? All

right, Godfather Drosselmeier, I'll tell you a thing or two. If your little

creatures in the castle always have to do the same thing, then I think

very little of them! I'd rather play with my soldiers. They can maneu~

ver backwards and forwards just like I tell them to, and they're not

locked away in a house."

With those words, Fritz moved away to the other table. There he

set his squadron of silver horsemen trotting here and there, wheeling and charging and slashing right and left to his heart's content. Marie had already slipped softly away, for she too was tired of the stately walking and dancing of the castle puppets. But, kind and gentle as she was, she did not wish to seem ungrateful in the way her brother had.

Somewhat annoyed, Godfather Drosselmeier said to their parents, "Well! Maybe an ingenious mechanism like this is not for children. I'll just put my castle back in its box."

Mama came to the rescue and made him show her the intricate machinery that moved all the figures. Drosselmeier took the whole thing apart, then put it together again. In the process, he entirely recovered his temper. Calm once more, he gave the children handfuls of gingerbread men and women with sweet golden faces, hands, and legs. These delighted the children.

Marie's Sweetheart

Marie wasn't ready to leave the display of   Christmas presents just yet, for she had no-

ticed something new. When Fritz's soldiers halted to the right of the tree, a very splendid little man had

become visible, standing unobtrusively, as if waiting until it was his turn to be seen.

You might have found fault with his figure. His body was too

tall and fat for his legs, which were short and skinny. And his head

was much too large for his body. The elegance of his costume, however,

made up for a great deal. It showed him to be a person of taste and cul-

tivation. He was wearing a purple military jacket with knobs and

braid all over, pantaloons of the same purple as the jacket, and the finest

boots ever seen on an officer, boots which fit his little legs as if they had

been painted on. It was strange, however, that for all this fine style he

wore over his shoulders a rather ridiculous short cloak that looked al-

most as if it were made of wood, and on his head a cap like a miner's.

But, in the little man's defense, Marie remembered that Godfather

Drosselmeier often showed up in the mornings wearing a terribly ugly

jacket and an awful-looking cap on his head. And Godfather Drosselmeier was wonderful to her.

Marie fell in love with this little man at first sight. She gazed
into his face and saw clearly that he had a very sweet personality. His
green eyes (which stuck, perhaps, a little farther out of his head than
was quite desirable) beamed up at her with kindness and good cheer.
His chin was set off with a tidy beard of white cotton, which was another one of his good features. This beard drew attention to the smile
that was always on his bright red lips.

"Oh, Papa dear!" Marie asked at last, "who gets that adorable
present behind the tree?"

"Well, that fellow is going to do plenty of good work for all
of you," was the answer. "He's going to crack nuts for you, and he's
going to belong to your older sister, Louise, just as much as to you and
Fritz."

As Dr. Stahlbaum lifted the end of the little man's peculiar
wooden cloak, the man opened his mouth wider and wider, displaying
two rows of very white, sharp teeth. Following her father's instruc-
tions, Marie put a nut into the open mouth, and–*k-nack*–he bit it in
two. The nutshells fell down and Marie took the kernel.

Papa explained that this charming little man belonged to the

Nutcracker family and was practicing the profession of his ancestors.

"Now, Marie," said Papa, "as our friend Nutcracker seems to have made such an impression on you, he will become your special responsibility—though, as I said, Louise and Fritz are to have the same rights to employ him as you do."

Marie took the little man into her arms at once and made him crack more nuts. But she was careful to pick out only the smallest, so he wouldn't have to strain himself by opening his mouth too terribly wide. Then Louise came, and he had to crack some nuts for her too. It was a duty he seemed glad to perform, for he kept on smiling graciously.

Meanwhile, Fritz had gotten a little tired after so much drilling and maneuvering, so he joined his sisters. He laughed uproariously at the funny little man, who (since Fritz naturally wanted his share of the nuts) was passed from hand to hand, and had to snap his mouth open and shut again and again. Fritz gave him all the biggest and hardest nuts he could find.

All at once there was a *crack–crack,* and three teeth fell out of the Nutcracker's mouth.

"Oh, my poor dear Nutcracker!" Marie cried, and she grabbed

him away from Fritz. The little man's lower jaw was now loose and wobbly.

"A fine servant he is!" said Fritz. "Calls himself a Nutcracker, yet he can't give a decent bite. He doesn't seem to know much about his business. Hand him over here, Marie! I'll keep him cracking nuts even if he loses all the rest of his teeth—and his jaw in the bargain. Then we'll see what he's good for!"

"No, no," said Marie, in tears. "You can't have him—my sweet Nutcracker! See how sadly he's looking at me, showing me his sore mouth. You're cruel, Fritz! You beat your horses, and I know for a fact that you've had one of your soldiers shot."

"Those things must be done," said Fritz, "and you don't understand anything about it. Nutcracker's as much mine as yours, so hand him over!"

Marie began to cry in earnest, and she quickly wrapped the wounded Nutcracker up in her little pocket handkerchief. Papa and Mama came with Godfather Drosselmeier, who took Fritz's side, much to Marie's distress. But then Papa said, "I put Nutcracker in Marie's special care, and he seems to need her now. She'll have full power over him, and nobody else can say a word about it. Why, I'm surprised that Fritz expects more service from a man wounded in the line of duty. As a good soldier, he ought to know better than that."

Fritz was ashamed, and he resolved not to spend any more time on nuts or nutcrackers. So he crept off to the other side of the table, where his soldiers (having established the necessary outposts) were encamped for the evening.

Marie collected Nutcracker's lost teeth, then took a soft white ribbon from her dress to wrap around his chin. Finally she wrapped Nutcracker, who was looking very pale and frightened, in her handkerchief even more tenderly than before. Rocking him like a child in her arms, she looked at the picture books again.

But she soon grew angry (which was not usual with her) at Godfather Drosselmeier. He kept laughing and asking her how she could make such a fuss about such an ugly little man.

Remember that, when Marie had first seen Nutcracker, she had been struck by the way he resembled Godfather Drosselmeier. The likeness now popped into her mind again. She said, very seriously, "Who knows, Godfather—if you were dressed the same as my darling Nutcracker, and had on the same shining boots—you might look almost as handsome as he does!"

Then Marie became confused. She could not understand why
Papa and Mama laughed so loud, or why Godfather Drosselmeier's
nose grew so red, or why he wasn't laughing as hard as before. She
decided that there was probably some special reason for all these
things.

Wonderful Events

As you go into the sitting-room in the Stahlbaums'  house, on your left-hand side you will see a tall glass cabinet set against the wall. All the children's toys are put away there for safekeeping. Louise, the elder

❄

sister, was still quite little when her father had this cabinet built. A very skillful craftsman used fine panes of glass

———◆◆◆◆◆———

which he fit together so artfully that everything the children put in-side looked more shining and lovely than they ever did in the children's hands.

The elaborate works of art that Drosselmeier made were stowed on the upper shelves, which Fritz and Marie could not reach. Immediately underneath, there was a shelf for the picture books. Fritz and Marie were allowed to do what they liked with the two bottom shelves. Marie claimed the lowest one of all for her dolls' residence, while Fritz bunked his troops on the one above.

On this Christmas Eve, Fritz set his soldiers on his shelf, while Marie pushed Miss Gertrude into a corner and settled her nice new doll in among the furniture on the bottom shelf. Then Marie invited herself to take tea and cakes with her dolls.

This bottom-shelf doll apartment was decorated with the utmost taste, everything being of the highest quality. I don't know if you, my attentive reader, have the satisfaction of possessing an equally well-appointed space for your dolls. Imagine, if you will, an apartment that featured a flowered sofa, a number of charming chairs, an elegant tea-table, and, above all, a cozy white bed where the pretty darlings could go to sleep. On the walls were hung beautiful little pictures. In such a delightful apartment as this, the new doll (whose name, Marie discovered, was Miss Klara) thought herself very comfortably settled.

It grew quite late—midnight was not far off, and Godfather Drosselmeier had long ago departed—before the children could tear themselves away from all these Christmas fascinations. They sat riveted beside the glass cabinet, and their mother had to remind them several times that it was well past bedtime.

"Yes, I'm sure these poor men are exhausted," Fritz said, meaning his soldiers. "They must be anxious to get some sleep. As long as I'm here, none of them dare to even blink their eyes." With those words, he went off to bed.

But Marie begged to stay up. "Just a little longer, a tiny little while longer, please, Mama! I still have a lot to arrange. As soon as everything is settled, I promise that I shall go straight to bed."

Marie was always a docile, reasonable child, so her mother let her stay with her toys a little longer. Suspecting that Marie might grow so absorbed in her new doll that she would forget to extinguish the candles that were burning in the wall sconces, Mama herself blew all of them out. Only the lamp that hung from the ceiling stayed on, giving a soft and pleasant light.

"Come to bed soon, Marie, or you'll never be up on time in the morning," Mama said as she went off to her own bedroom.

As soon as Marie was alone, she set rapidly to work at what she wanted most to do. Though she couldn't have said why, this was something that she had not wanted to do in her mother's presence. She had been holding Nutcracker in one arm all this time, and now she laid him softly on the table, gently unrolled the handkerchief, and examined his wounds.

Nutcracker was very pale, but at the same time he smiled with a melancholy gentleness that went straight to Marie's heart.

"Oh, my darling little Nutcracker!" she said softly. "Please don't be upset because my brother hurt you like this. He didn't mean to, you

know. He's gotten a little harsh because of his soldiering and all that, but I promise you he's really a nice boy. I'll take such good care of you~ I'll nurse you till you're completely better. I'll have your teeth put in again, and your shoulder set properly. Godfather Drosselmeier will see to it. He knows how to do things~"

But Marie did not finish her sentence, because at the mention of Godfather Drosselmeier, her friend Nutcracker made a horrible face. A sort of sharp green lightning seemed to dart out of his eyes.

This lasted only an instant, however. Just as Marie began to grow frightened, she found that she was looking at the very same kind face, with its gentle smile, that she had been gazing at before. She decided that the change had been caused by some breeze that had made the lamp flicker.

"Well!" she said, "I certainly am silly to be scared so easily, and to think that a wooden doll could make faces at me! I really do love Nutcracker, because he's so funny and sweet. I have to take the very best care of him until he's well and happy again."

Then she took him in her arms, approached the cabinet, knelt down beside it, and said to her new doll, "I'm going to ask a favor of you, Miss Klara. Please give up your bed to this poor, sick, wounded Nutcracker, and make yourself as comfortable as you can on the sofa.

Remember that you're well and strong yourself, or you wouldn't have such fat red cheeks. Remember too that there are very few dolls who have as comfortable a sofa as this to lie upon."

Miss Klara sat there in her Christmas finery, looking very grand and disdainful. She wouldn't say so much as "Boo!"

"Very well," said Marie. "Why should I make such a fuss and stand on any ceremony at all?" She took the bed, moved it forward, and laid Nutcracker tenderly down upon it. Then she took a ribbon from her own dress to wrap around his hurt shoulder. Finally, she drew the blankets up to his nose.

"He won't stay with that nasty Klara," she said. She moved the small bed, with Nutcracker in it, to the shelf above, so that it rested near the village in which Fritz's soldiers had their encampments. She closed the cabinet and moved away to go to bed, then—

Listen!

Very lightly, very slowly, a noise arose. It whispered and rustled and crept. It was all around her, in all directions, coming from every corner of the room—from underneath the stove, under the chairs, behind the cabinets.

The clock on the wall ticked loudly, then louder still, warning that it was about to strike the hour. But it didn't strike. Marie saw that the big gilt owl on its top had dropped its wings so that they covered

the whole clock. The owl stretched its catlike head, with its crooked

beak, a long way forward. The ticking kept growing louder and louder

until it formed distinct words:

Clocks clocking, clocking clocks,

Make no sound but soft tick-tocks.

Mouse King has a fine-tuned ear–

Prr prr, pum pum.

Sing an ancient song of fear–

Prr prr, pum pum.

Now strike, you clocks, strike loud!

He's coming soon, just as he vowed!

Then the clock croaked hollowly–*Pum! Pum!*–twelve times.

Marie was terrified. She was ready to run away as fast as she

could. But then she noticed that instead of the owl it was Godfather

Drosselmeier on top of the clock, with his yellow coattails hanging

down on both sides like wings.

Quickly she steeled herself and called out in a loud voice, "Godfather! Godfather Drosselmeier! What are you up there for? Come down here and don't scare me like that, you naughty man!"

Suddenly there began a sort of wild cheeping and squeaking everywhere, and sounds of running and scampering, as if there were thousands of little feet behind the walls. Hundreds of lights began to glitter out through chinks in the woodwork. But they were not lights— no, no! They were tiny glittering eyes!

Marie saw at last that mice were peeping everywhere, squeez- ing out through every crack. Soon they were trotting and galloping all over the room. These were organized bodies of mice, steadily increas- ing, forming themselves into regular troops and squadrons, just as Fritz's soldiers had done when he was conducting maneuvers.

Since Marie was not afraid of mice (as many children are), she could not help being amused. But suddenly there came such a sharp and terrible piping noise that the blood ran cold in her veins.

And *then* what did she see?

Dear reader, I know that you are brave of heart, but if you had seen what now came before Marie's eyes, you would have run off as fast as lightning straight into your bed and drawn the blankets way over your head.

Poor Marie had no chance to run, however. For right at her feet, as if pushed by some subterranean power, there burst up a shower of sand, lime, and broken stone. Seven mouse heads with seven shining crowns upon them rose through the floor, hissing and piping in a most horrible way. All of these seven crowned heads belonged to a single large body which now forced its way up through the floor as well.

This enormous creature, the Mouse King, squeaked to the assembled multitude with all seven of its mouths in full chorus. Then the entire mouse army set itself in motion. It trot-trotted right up to the cabinet—and up to Marie, who was still standing there beside it.

Marie's heart had been beating so hard with terror that she thought it would burst from her chest. Looking at the Mouse King, she felt her heart stop. Half-fainting, she swayed backward.

Suddenly she heard a *clink, clink, crr*—her elbow had broken a pane of the cabinet, and shards of broken glass fell to the floor, tinkling as they shattered. She felt for a moment a sharp, stinging pain in her arm, but this seemed only to make her heart lighter. She heard no more of the squeaking and piping. Everything was quiet. Though she didn't dare to look, she hoped that the noise of the breaking glass had frightened the mice back into their holes.

But what happened next? Behind Marie, a movement arose in the cabinet, and small, faint voices began to be heard:

❀

Wake up, wake up! It's time to fight—

The battle starts this very night!

Wake up, wake up—and fight! And fight!

❀

Now tiny bells began to ring.

"Oh! that's my music box!" cried Marie. She crouched down and saw that a bright light had arisen within the cabinet, setting all the toys in sudden motion. Dolls and figurines of all kinds were running about and struggling with tiny weapons. At this point, Nutcracker rose from his bed, cast off the blankets, and sprang with both feet onto the shelf, shouting at the top of his voice:

❀

K-nack, k-nack, k-nack,

Stupid mousey pack,

Stupid chitter-chat!

K-nack, k-nack, crick and crack,

Your skulls are going to crack!

❀

With this he drew his little sword, waved it in the air, and cried, "My trusty friends and followers! Are you ready to stand by me in this battle?"

Immediately a response came forth from three swordfighting Italian clowns and their father, Pantaloon, as well as four chimneysweeps, two zither-players, and a drummer: "Yes, Your Highness! We'll stand by you! We'll follow you to battle, whether it brings victory or death!" They flung themselves after Nutcracker, who, in the excitement of the moment, had already made a perilous leap to the bottom shelf.

As for the clowns and the rest of the Nutcracker's followers, the risk of this leap was not so great. After all, they were not only amply clothed, but they also were padded by soft insides made of cotton and sawdust. As a result, they plunked down like little beanbags. But poor Nutcracker would certainly have broken his arms and legs, for it was nearly two feet to the bottom shelf and his body was made of fragile wood if Miss Klara hadn't prevented a dangerous landing by catching the hero, drawn sword and all, in her tender arms.

"Oh, you dear, good Klara!" cried Marie. "How could I have misunderstood you so? I had thought that you were too uncaring to let dear Nutcracker have your bed."

Miss Klara now exclaimed, as she pressed the young hero gently to her silken breast, "Oh, my lord! Don't enter this dangerous battle, sick and wounded as you are. See how your trusty followers, the clowns, chimneysweeps, zithermen, and drummer, are already lined up below. Even the puzzle-figures on my shelf are preparing for the fray! My dear lord, rest here in my arms and observe your victory from a safe location."

Nutcracker refused to hold himself back. He kicked about with his legs until Klara was obliged to release him. But then, to be certain that she understood how grateful he was for her kindness, Nutcracker sank gracefully to one knee and said: "Oh, lady! The kind protection and aid that you have offered me will forever gladden my heart, in battle and in victory!"

At these words, Klara bowed and took hold of Nutcracker by his arms. She raised him up gently and then loosened her sash, which was ornamented with many spangles. Her plan was to drape it around his shoulders. But the little man swiftly took two steps back, laid his hand upon his heart, and said, with much solemnity, "Oh, lady! Do not give this mark of your favor to me, for—" He hesitated and gave a deep sigh. Then he took from his shoulders the ribbon with which Marie had bandaged him and pressed it to his lips. He put it back on as a token that he was fighting for Marie. Waving his glittering sword, he sprang

like a bird over the ledge of the cabinet down to the floor.

You will recall, dear reader, that even before Nutcracker had

come completely to life, he had felt Marie's great love and concern for

him. How, then, could he possibly have accepted Miss Klara's sash—no

matter how elegant it was? The faithful little man preferred Marie's

much commoner and less pretentious token.

At the very moment Nutcracker sprang down, the squeaking

and piping began again worse than ever. Underneath the big table, the

mouse army had massed itself, taking its orders from the terrible

Mouse King with his seven heads.

The battle was about to begin.

the attle

"Beat the victory march, trusty drummer!" cried Nutcracker. Immediately the little soldier began to strike a

drumroll in such a splendid style that the windows of the glass cabinet rattled and resounded. A cracking

and a clattering arose, and Marie saw that 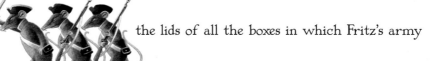 the lids of all the boxes in which Fritz's army

was quartered were bursting open. The soldiers all poured out and

jumped down to the bottom shelf, where they lined up in battle forma-

tions. Nutcracker quickly inspected the ranks, speaking words both of

encouragement and reproof.

"Why is there no trumpeter amongst you sounding out a call?"

he cried in a fury.

Then he turned to the old Italian clown, Pantaloon. Looking

somewhat pale, with his hurt chin wobbling, Nutcracker said ceremo-

niously, "I know how brave and experienced you are, General. What we

need now is someone who can size up situations rapidly and make the

most of every opportunity. I therefore entrust you with the command

of the cavalry and artillery. You can do without a horse. Your own legs are long and you can gallop upon them as fast as you need to. Now do your duty!"

Immediately Pantaloon put his long, lean fingers to his mouth and whistled so sharply that it seemed as if a hundred trumpets were blaring. Sounds of stamping and neighing now issued forth from the cabinet. Fritz's dragoons and swordsmen—along with his shiny new soldiers—marched out and lined up on the floor. They trooped past Nutcracker in regiments, banners flying and bands playing. After this maneuver, they wheeled and formed up at right angles to the line of the march, while Fritz's artillery came rolling into position at the front.

At once the cannons commenced to fire—boom-boom-boom! Marie saw sugarplum ammunition wreaking havoc among the thickly massed mouse battalions, covering them with white sugar-powder. A division of heavy guns, which had taken a strong position on Mama's footstool, did the greatest work—*bam-bam-bam!* They kept up a murderous fire of gingerbread nuts on the enemy's ranks, mowing the mice down in dozens.

But the advance of the enemy mice was scarcely slowed by all this. They even seized control of one or two of the heavy guns—when suddenly there came a *prr-prr-prr!* Marie could hardly see what was happening with all the smoke and dust. Soldiers on both sides fought with the utmost bravery and determination, and it was uncertain for a long time which side would win the day. The mice kept on adding fresh forces to their ranks and advancing to the front. Their little silver musketballs were everywhere, doing terrible damage even inside the glass cabinet.

Klara and Gertrude ran around desperately, wringing their hands and crying out in distress.

"Must I—the loveliest doll in the world—die miserably in the flower of my youth?" wailed Miss Klara.

"Did I take such care of myself all these years, to be shot down within my own four walls?" wept Gertrude.

They fell into each other's arms and howled so terribly that you could hear them even above the din of battle. Dear reader, you have no idea of the pandemonium! It was all *prr-prr-poof, boom-booroom, boom-booroom, boom!* The Mouse King and his army squeaked and screamed. Above all this din, Nutcracker's powerful voice could be heard shouting commands as he strode among his battalions in the thick of the fire.

Meanwhile, General Pantaloon had made several brilliant cavalry charges and covered himself with glory. Fritz's soldiers, however, were subjected to a barrage of evil-smelling shot that left deadly marks on their red tunics, and so they hung back from the battle. General

Pantaloon ordered them to wheel around to the left. In the excitement

of the moment, however, he ordered his dragoons and swordsmen to do

likewise. And so they too wheeled to the left and marched home to

their quarters.

This mistaken maneuver brought the artillery on the footstool

into imminent danger. It was not long before a large troop of hideous

mice assaulted them so efficiently that the whole of the footstool, with

its guns and gunners, fell into the enemy's hands.

Nutcracker was very upset, and he ordered his right wing to

begin a backward movement. A soldier of your experience, my dear

reader, knows that such a movement is almost the same as a retreat.

Perhaps, then, you can anticipate the disaster about to befall the army

of Marie's beloved little Nutcracker.

But just look a bit in the other direction, at the left wing under

Nutcracker's command. There all is going well and we still have reason

for hope. During the hottest part of the fighting, masses of mouse cav-

alry had quietly advanced from under the chest of drawers. With loud,

horrible squeaks they struck at this left wing.

What a fierce reception they met! Very slowly (for they had to

edge along at the bottom of the cabinet), the regiment of puzzle figures appeared—brightly dressed gardeners, mountain climbers, snake charmers, hairdressers, harlequins, Cupids, lions, tigers, unicorns, and monkeys, all under the command of two Chinese emperors. They strode into battle and formed a square, fighting with the utmost courage and coolness.

This elite regiment would have seized victory from the enemy if one of the mouse cavalry captains hadn't made a bold push forward. He charged upon one of the Chinese emperors and bit off his head. As the emperor fell, he knocked over and smothered a couple of harlequins and a unicorn. These losses created a gap through which the mouse enemy rushed. Tragically, the whole puzzle-figure regiment was soon bitten to death.

In the end, however, the mice gained little advantage from this victory. For as soon as one of the mouse cavalry soldiers bit a brave puzzle-figure soldier to death, he found himself choking from the thick cardboard that stuck in his throat. Still, these mouse fatalities proved of little good to Nutcracker's army, which was forced to retreat farther and farther, while suffering greater and greater losses. The unfortunate Nutcracker soon found himself driven back to the glass cabinet, with a very small remnant of his army remaining.

Nutcracker was counting on reinforcements from within the

cabinet. "Bring up the reserves!" he shouted. "General Pantaloon! Swordfighters! Drummers! Where the devil are you?"

In response, a small contingent of brown gingerbread men and women with gilt faces, hats, and helmets appeared. But they flailed their arms about so clumsily that they never hit any of the enemy. All they succeeded in doing was to knock off the cap of their commander, Nutcracker himself. Soon the mice bit their gingerbread legs off, and they tumbled topsy-turvy, killing several of Nutcracker's remaining soldiers as they fell.

Nutcracker was now hemmed in by the enemy and in a position of extreme danger. He tried to jump up onto the bottom ledge of the cabinet, but his legs were not long enough. Unfortunately, Klara and Gertrude fainted so they could give him no assistance. Heavy dragoons from the mouse army came charging at him, and Nutcracker shouted wildly, "A horse! A horse! My kingdom for a horse!"

Just then, two mouse riflemen seized him by his wooden cloak. The Mouse King came rushing up to him, screeching out in triumph from all seven of his throats.

Marie could contain herself no longer. "Oh, my poor Nutcracker!" she sobbed. Without really knowing what she was doing, she took her left shoe off and threw it as hard as she could into the thick

of the enemy—straight at the Mouse King.

Instantly everything vanished.

Then the pain in Marie's left arm grew sharper, and she fell to

the floor unconscious.

———◆◆◆———

the Invalid

When Marie awoke from a long deathlike sleep, she was lying in her bed. Soft, translucent sunlight outlined the del-

icate frost flowers which covered the window. A gentleman was sitting beside her, and after a

moment she recognized him as the children's doctor, Wendelstern. "She's awake," he said in a soft voice, and Marie's

mother came and looked anxiously into her face.

"Oh, Mother!" whispered Marie, "have all those awful mice

gone away, and is the good Nutcracker all right?"

"Don't talk such nonsense, sweetheart," her mother answered.

"Mice have nothing to do with our Nutcracker. You naughty girl—

you've driven us out of our minds with worry. See what happens when

children don't do as they're told! You were playing with your toys so

late last night that you became very sleepy. Now, I don't know whether

or not some mouse jumped out and frightened you, though we usually

don't have a problem with mice. But I do know that you broke a pane of

the glass cabinet with your elbow. You cut your arm so badly that Dr.

Wendelstern, who has just removed a number of glass shards from your arm, thinks that if the cut had been just a little higher up, you might have had a stiff arm for life or even bled to death. Thank heaven I woke up in the middle of the night and wondered about you. When I came down the stairs I found you lying unconscious in front of the cabinet, bleeding frightfully, with all sorts of toys—Fritz's lead soldiers, broken puzzle figures, gingerbread men—scattered around you. Nutcracker was lying on your bleeding arm, with your left shoe not far off."

"Oh, Mama," said Marie, "you saw what was left from an enormous battle between the toys and the mice. What scared me so much was that the mice were going to hurt Nutcracker—who was the commander of the toy army. To protect him, I threw my shoe at the mice, and after that I don't know what else happened."

Dr. Wendelstern winked meaningfully at Marie's mother, who said very gently, "Never mind, dear. The mice have all gone away now, and Nutcracker's in the cabinet, safe and sound."

In a little while, Marie's father came and had a long consultation with Dr. Wendelstern. Then Papa himself felt Marie's pulse. Marie heard the grown-ups mention "wound fever." She would have to stay in bed and take medicine for a few days, even though she didn't feel very ill, aside from the pain and stiffness in her arm.

Marie was very thankful that Nutcracker had survived the battle safe and sound. She seemed to remember, as if in a dream, that he had said—quite distinctly in a melancholy voice—"Marie, dearest lady, I am deeply indebted to you. And it is in your power to do even more for me..."

She wondered what his words could possibly mean, but they remained a mystery to her.

Because of her arm, Marie couldn't play as usual. When she tried to read her picture books, everything wavered before her eyes so strangely that she had to stop. The days grew very long for her. Her spirits rose in the evenings, when her mother would sit by her bed and read her pleasant stories.

One night, Mama had just finished reading a story about a prince named Fakardin when the door opened and in came Godfather Drosselmeier. "I've come to see with my own eyes how Marie is doing," he explained.

When Marie saw Godfather Drosselmeier in his little yellow coat, a vivid memory arose within her of the night Nutcracker lost the battle against the mice. "Oh, Godfather Drosselmeier, you were so cruel!" she couldn't help crying out. "I saw you sitting on the clock, covering it up with your wings so that it wouldn't strike the hour and scare the mice. I heard you when you called the Mouse King. Why didn't you help Nutcracker? Why didn't you help *me*, you nasty godfather? Do you realize it's your fault that I'm lying here with a bad arm?"

Her mother, greatly alarmed, demanded, "What's wrong with you, Marie?"

Drosselmeier made some strange faces. Then he chanted in a snarling monotone:

❀

Clockworks only buzzed and stuck;

Tick-tick-tick went all the clocks.

Not allowed to chime the hour,

They only buzzed a warning dour.

Then rang the bell a loud *kling-klang–*

Bing and *bong* and *bong* and *bang–*

Maiden dolls, don't be afraid!

The battle's done, Nutcracker saved!

Now comes the owl on stealthy wing;

Scares away the mean Mouse King.

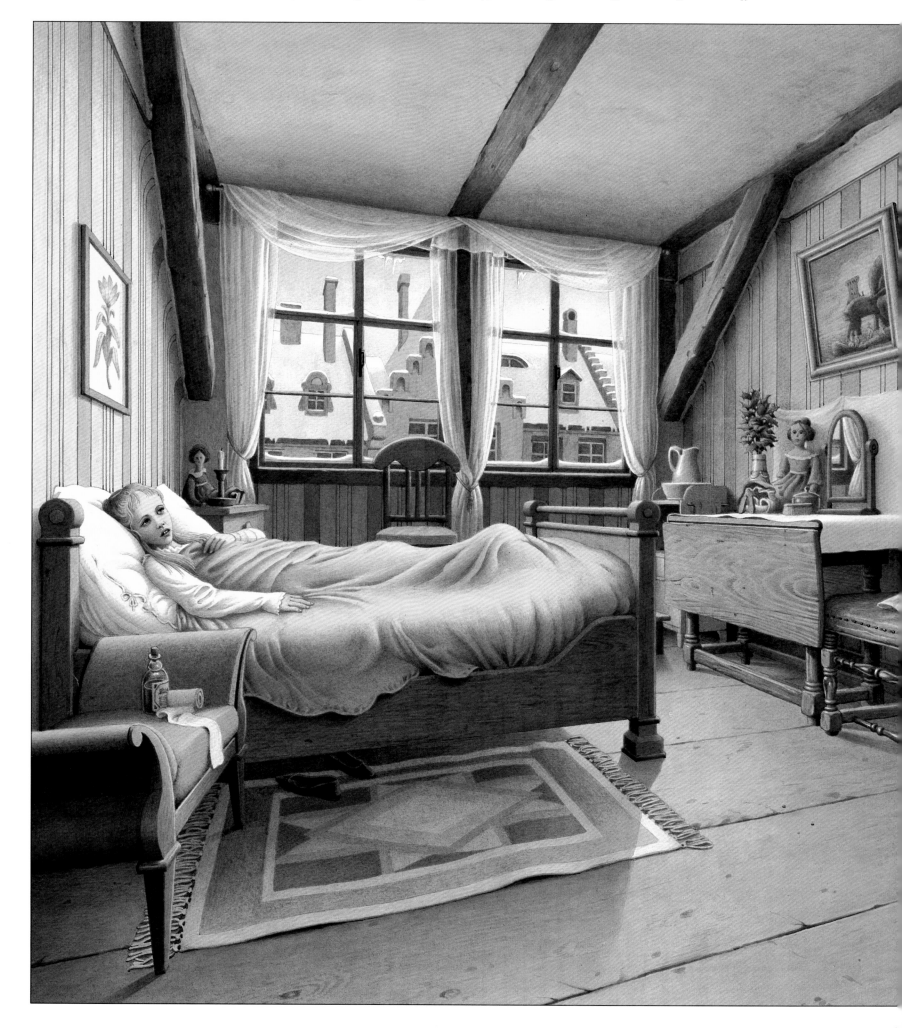

Buzz and *tick* and *hum* and *boom*–

Clocks tock again and time resumes.

Tick and *tock* and *grr* and *brr*–

Marie's afraid they're after her.

❀

Marie's eyes grew wide with fear as she gazed at Godfather Drosselmeier. He looked even more ugly than usual, jerking his right arm back and forth like a clock's pendulum, or like a puppet on a string. She grew terribly afraid of him, though Fritz (who had arrived during Drosselmeier's chant) only laughed and said, "Oh, Godfather, look at you, hopping around like that! You look like the old jumping jack I threw away last month."

Mama looked very serious and said, "This is a very strange way of behaving, Mr. Drosselmeier. What do you mean by it?"

"My goodness!" said Drosselmeier, laughing. "Haven't you ever heard my nice 'Song of the Clockmaker'? I always sing it to little invalids like Marie." He sat down beside Marie's bed and whispered to her, "Don't be annoyed with me because I didn't gouge out all fourteen of the Mouse King's eyes. I couldn't do that. To make up for it, here's something that I know will make you happy."

He dug into one of his pockets, and slowly, slowly he pulled out–Nutcracker! His teeth and his broken jaw had been firmly fixed. Marie shouted for joy, and her mother laughed and said, "Now you see for yourself how nice Godfather Drosselmeier is to Nut-cracker."

"Even so, Marie," said Drosselmeier, "Nutcracker is still far from handsome. If you'd like, I'll tell you how it was that ugliness first came into his family. Did you ever hear of the Princess Pirlipat, the witch Dame Mouserinks, and the clever Clockmaker?"

"Listen here, Godfather Drosselmeier," Fritz interrupted. "You've put Nutcracker's teeth in all right, and his jaw isn't as wobbly as it was. But why haven't you given him a sword?"

"Boy," said Drosselmeier, irritated, "you're always finding fault with something or other! What have I got to do with Nutcracker's sword? I've fixed his mouth for him. He'll have to find a sword for himself."

"Yes, yes," Fritz replied. "And he will, of course, if he's a decent sort of person."

"So tell me, Marie," Drosselmeier continued. "Do you know the story of Princess Pirlipat?"

"No," said Marie. "Tell it to me, please!"

"I hope it won't be as strange and terrible as your stories generally are," said her mother to Drosselmeier.

"Nothing of the kind," he answered. "On the contrary, the story I have the honor of telling you this time is actually very funny."

"Go on, then—tell it to us," begged the children.

Drosselmeier commenced as follows:

———◆◆◆◆———

the Story of the Hard Nut

Pirlipat's mother was a king's wife, which meant that she was a queen. Pirlipat herself became a princess the moment

she was born. The king was quite beside him-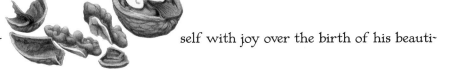self with joy over the birth of his beauti-

ful little daughter. As she lay in her cradle, he danced gleefully about on one leg, shouting out again and again, "Hip!

Hurrah! Hurrah! Hip, hip, hurrah! Did anybody ever see anything so

lovely as my little Pirlipat?"

All the ministers of state, as well as the generals, the presidents,

and the officers of the staff, danced about on one leg as the king did.

They cried out in response, "No, no–never!"

Indeed, there was no denying that since the world began there

had never been a lovelier baby than Princess Pirlipat. Her little face

looked as if it had been woven out of the most delicate white- and rose-

colored silk. Her eyes were of sparkling azure, and her hair resembled

curling threads of gold. Moreover, she had come into the world with two rows of little pearly teeth—with which, two hours after her birth, she bit the Lord High Chancellor, making him shout, "Oh Gemini!" quite loudly. Fierce as this bite was, it pleased the people of the kingdom, who felt that it showed great intelligence and discrimination on the part of the angelical little baby.

All was joy and gladness, except for one thing. The queen was very anxious and uneasy, though nobody could tell why. She insisted that Pirlipat's cradle be very carefully guarded. Not only did she keep soldiers at the nursery doors, but she also stationed two head nurses next to the cradle, with six other nurses posted around the room at night. But what seemed strangest of all was that these nurses were required to have cats on their laps and to pet them all night long, so that they would never stop purring.

Dear reader, now let me explain how all these strange precautions came about.

Once upon a time, many powerful kings and princes assembled at the court of Pirlipat's father. To entertain these great nobles, tournaments, plays, and formal balls were held on the grandest scale. The king, who wished to exhibit his great wealth, made up his mind that for once he would draw even more deeply from the royal treasury. To impress his guests to the utmost, he decided to give a grand sausage

banquet. After having checked both with the master cook and the court astronomer to find an hour appropriate for pork butchering, he jumped into a state carriage and personally invited all the kings and princes to a meal. He told them that the menu would consist solely of soup, because he wanted to surprise them with the magnificence of his sausages.

Upon his return to the palace, he said to the queen, very graciously, "My darling, only *you* know exactly how I like my sausages!"

The queen understood that this meant that she would have to make the sausages herself. She promptly ordered the chancellor of the treasury to take the great golden sausage kettle and the silver casserole dishes out of storage. An enormous fire was kindled out of sandalwood, the queen put on her damask kitchen apron, and, with the help of a few ladies-in-waiting, a delicious aroma of broth was soon steaming out of the kettle.

This tantalizing smell penetrated into the state council chamber. The king could not control himself. "Excuse me for a few minutes, my lords and gentlemen," he said. He rushed into the kitchen, embraced the queen, stirred the kettle with his own golden scepter, and then returned to the council chamber with a peaceful mind.

Now the crucial moment arrived for cutting the fat into little pieces and browning it on silver spits. The ladies-in-waiting retired because the queen, out of love and respect for her royal husband, wanted to do the rest of the work herself.

While she was working alone, the queen suddenly heard, as the fat began to brown, a delicate whispering voice that was saying, "Psst, sister! Give me some of that! I'm a queen just like you."

The queen knew well who was speaking. It was the witch Dame Mouserinks, who had resided in the palace for many years. She was queen of the realm of Mousolia and she lived with a considerable court of her own under the kitchen hearth. She even claimed to be related to the royal family of the king and queen.

Pirlipat's mother was a kind-hearted woman. Though she didn't care to recognize Dame Mouserinks as a relative, she was willing, at this festive season, to spare the tidbits that Dame Mouserinks requested. So she said, "Come out, then, Dame Mouserinks. Of course you can taste my browned fat."

Dame Mouserinks came running out as fast as she could, held up her dainty little paws, and took one morsel of fat after another as quickly as the queen held them out.

The queen's charity couldn't stop there. Soon all Dame Mouserinks's uncles and cousins and aunts scurried into the kitchen, as did her seven sons, all dull-witted rascals. They all demanded their share of browned fat, and the queen was too frightened to refuse them. Luckily, the head lady-in-waiting came in and she drove the demanding visitors away. Thus a little of the browned fat was left over. Filled with worry, the queen called in the court mathematician, who skillfully devised a formula by which the remaining fat could be evenly distributed among all the remaining sausages.

The next evening, kettledrums and trumpets summoned the foreign princes and rulers to the feast. They arrived wearing their robes of state, some of them on white palfreys, some in coaches made of glass. The king received them with much gracious ceremony and took his seat at the head of the table, with his crown on his head and his scepter in his hand.

But as the liverwurst sausage course was being served, some guests observed that the king was turning pale and raising his eyes to heaven. His bosom was heaving in terrific sighs, and it was clear that some terrible pain was assaulting his insides. When the blood sausages were handed around, he fell back in his seat, covered his face with his hands, and loudly wailed and groaned.

The guests all sprang from the table and the court physician groped desperately for the unlucky ruler's pulse. A nameless sorrow

seemed to be weighing on him. At last, after the doctor had tried every remedy he could think of–burning feathers under the king's nose, and so on–the royal patient seemed to come around a bit. He stammered, barely audibly, the words, "Too little fat!"

The queen threw herself at his feet in despair and cried, in a voice broken by sobs, "Oh, my poor unhappy royal husband! What pain you must be feeling! See the guilty one here at your feet! Dame Mouserinks and all her family, they came and gobbled up the fat and–"

With these words, the queen fainted.

The king jumped up, full of fury, and cried in a terrible voice, "Lady, what is the meaning of this?"

The head lady-in-waiting told all she knew, and the king swore to take revenge on Dame Mouserinks and her family for devouring the fat that was meant for the sausages. The privy council was summoned, and it proclaimed that Dame Mouserinks should be put on trial and that all her property should be seized. To prevent her from eating any more of the fat that rightfully belonged to him, the king called in the court clockmaker whose name was the same as mine–Christian Elias Drosselmeier.

The clockmaker promised that he would rid the palace of

Dame Mouserinks and her family once and for all, by means of crafty diplomacy. He invented very small and clever mousetrap chambers, into which pieces of browned fat were inserted. He placed these chambers all around the home of Dame Fatgobbler, as Mouserinks was now known. Mouserinks herself was much too smart not to see through Drosselmeier's scheme; but her efforts to warn her relatives of the danger were useless. Lured by the tantalizing smell of fat, all seven of her sons and a great many of her uncles, cousins, and aunts walked into Drosselmeier's little chambers and were immediately taken prisoners by the fall of a small gate. Once trapped, they were carried to the kitchen to meet their shameful fate. With the small remaining portion of her entourage, Dame Mouserinks fled this scene of horror. Sorrow and rage filled her breast.

The court rejoiced greatly, though the queen was worried. She knew Dame Mouserinks all too well, and understood that the Mouse Queen—with her powers of witchcraft—would never allow the death of her sons and other relatives to go unavenged. One day, while the queen was cooking fricasseed sheep's lungs for the king (a dish he especially enjoyed), Dame Mouserinks suddenly appeared and said, "My sons and my uncles, my cousins and my aunts, are now no more. Be

careful, lady, or the queen of the mice will bite your little princess in two!"

With these words, she vanished. The queen was so frightened that she dropped the fricassee into the fire. This was now the second time that Dame Mouserinks had spoiled one of the king's favorite dishes, which made him even angrier.

But that's enough for tonight, children; the rest will wait for later . . .

No matter how earnestly Marie begged Godfather Drosselmeier to go on with the story, he wouldn't. He jumped up, saying, "Too much at a time wouldn't be good for you. You'll get the rest tomorrow."

Marie had her own ideas about the story, but she understood that she would have to wait.

Just as the clockmaker was crossing over the threshold, Fritz shouted, "Tell us, Godfather Drosselmeier, was it really you who invented the mousetraps?"

"How can you ask such silly questions?" cried his mother.

Drosselmeier laughed oddly and said, "Well, don't you think I'm a good clockmaker—and shouldn't a good clockmaker know how to make a good mousetrap?"

The Story of the Hard Nut, Continued

❁

Now you understand, children (said Godfather Drosselmeier the next evening), why it was that the queen took such measures to guard her precious little Pirlipat. She was constantly afraid that Dame Mouserinks would come back and carry out her threat to bite the princess to death!

Remember Drosselmeier's ingenious mousetraps were of no use against the clever and cunning Dame Mouserinks. The court astrologer determined that only the Cat Purr family had the power to keep her away. This explains why each of the nurses had to keep a descendant of that family (all of whom had been given the honorary rank and title of Privy Councilors) on her lap and to keep him awake through the dark hours by gently scratching his back.

One night, just after midnight, one of the chief nurses stationed close to the cradle woke from a deep nap. Everything around her lay imprisoned in sleep—no purring, just a deep, deathlike silence that made a beetle scrabbling inside the wall sound quite loud.

Suddenly this head nurse saw, right before her eyes, a huge, hideous mouse, standing on its hind legs, with its head laid on the face of the tiny princess. The head nurse sprang up, screaming in horror!

Everybody woke up at the shriek. But Dame Mouserinks (for she was the great big mouse in Pirlipat's cradle) ran quickly away to the corner of the room. The Privy Councilors dashed after her, but too late! She was off and away through a chink in the floor.

The noise awoke Pirlipat, and she gave a miserable wail.

"Heaven be thanked!" cried all the nurses. "She's alive!"

Imagine their grief, however, when they looked at Pirlipat and saw what the beautiful, delicate little thing had become. An enormous bloated head (instead of the pretty little golden-haired one) sat at the top of a shrunken, crumpled-up body. Green, lifeless eyes stared out where the lovely azure blue pair had been, while her mouth had stretched from one ear to the other.

Of course, the queen nearly died of weeping and lamentation. The walls of the king's study had to be hung with padded tapestries, because he kept banging his head against them, shouting, "Oh, what a miserable king I am! Oh, what a miserable king!"

Naturally, this should have been the moment for him to decide that it would be much better to eat his sausages with no fat in them and to let Dame Mouserinks and her subjects remain peacefully under their hearthstone. But Pirlipat's royal father didn't think of it. What he did was to lay all the blame on the court clockmaker, Christian Elias Drosselmeier of Nuremberg. Which is why the king drafted a decree stating that within the space of four weeks Drosselmeier had to restore Princess Pirlipat to her original condition—or, at the least, to describe a sure way of doing so—or else suffer a shameful death by the executioner's ax.

Drosselmeier was more than a little alarmed. Yet he retained confidence in his art and in his luck. So he tried the first operation that seemed promising to him: He took Princess Pirlipat very carefully apart, screwed off her hands and feet, and examined her interior structure. Unfortunately, he found that as she grew bigger she would also grow more deformed.

He reassembled her carefully and then sank down beside her cradle—which he wasn't allowed to leave anyway—deeply depressed.

At last, the fourth week arrived. On the Wednesday of that week, the king came in with eyes gleaming with anger, waved his scepter about, and cried, "Christian Elias Drosselmeier, heal the princess or prepare to die!"

Drosselmeier began to weep bitterly while little Princess Pirlipat kept herself happy by cracking nuts.

For the first time, the clockmaker was struck by Pirlipat's remarkable appetite for nuts and by the unusual fact that she had come
into the world with her teeth already in place. He remembered that,
immediately after her transformation by the bite of Dame Mouserinks, she had gone on crying until by chance she was given a nut. She
had immediately cracked it open and eaten the kernel, then became
quite peaceful. From that moment on, her attendants were never able to
bring enough nuts to satisfy her.

"Oh, holy instinct of nature!" cried Drosselmeier. "You are the
force that relates all life. And now you have opened the door of this
mystery for me!"

He at once begged for permission to speak with the court
astrologer and was led to him, closely guarded. The two men embraced
each other in tears, for they were close friends. After a moment, they
withdrew into a private office, where they leafed through many books
about instinct, sympathy, antipathy, and other mysterious subjects.
Night fell. The court astrologer consulted the stars, and with
Drosselmeier's help (for the clockmaker also was an expert on astrol-
ogy) he drew up the princess's horoscope. This was a Herculean task, as
the astral lines kept tangling with each other. But at last—hurrah!—it
was clear: In order to break the witchy spell that had made her so ugly,

and thus regain her former beauty, Princess Pirlipat had to nibble on the kernel of the sweet nut Krakatuk.

Now, Krakatuk had such a hard shell that you could have fired a forty-eight-pound cannonball at it without cracking it in the slightest. Nonetheless, for the spell to be broken, this hard nut would have to be broken between the teeth of a man who had never shaved and who had never worn boots. Furthermore, he would have to do it in front of the princess. He would have to hand the kernel to her himself, and then take seven steps backwards without stumbling—with his eyes closed.

For three days and three nights, Drosselmeier and the astrologer worked without stopping. On Saturday, the king was sitting at his noonday meal when Drosselmeier—who was to be beheaded early Sunday morning—burst in full of joy and jubilation to explain the means by which he could restore the perfect beauty of Princess Pirlipat.

The king embraced him in a flood of rapture and promised him a diamond sword, four medals, and two new Sunday suits.

"Right after dinner," the monarch declared kindly, "you must get back to work. And be careful, dear clockmaker, that the young unshaven man in shoes, with the nut Krakatuk, is close at hand. Also, be sure that he drinks no wine before he comes. I don't want him to trip up when—crab-like—he takes his seven backward steps. He can get completely pickled afterwards, of course!"

Drosselmeier was dismayed at this speech by the king. He stammered, with considerable trembling, that the cure had only just been discovered. He still had to look both for the nut Krakatuk and for the young gentleman who was to crack it. Indeed, there was some doubt as to whether they could be found at all.

The king, enraged, whirled his scepter about his crowned head and roared like a lion, "All right, then—off with your head!"

It was lucky for poor, anxious Drosselmeier that the king had very much liked his meals that day and so was in a generous mood. Thus he was willing to listen to the queen, who made a very practical plea on the clockmaker's behalf.

Drosselmeier took courage from this plea and explained that he really had done the job assigned to him—to find the means to heal the princess. Thus he thought he had won the right to live.

At first, the king called this argument pure nonsense and empty chatter, but finally—after he'd had a dose of digestive medicine to soothe his stomach—he declared that the clockmaker and the astrologer should search ceaselessly until they had found the nut Krakatuk.

As for the man who was to crack the nut, the queen suggested that he could be located through advertisements placed in newspapers both at home and abroad.

Godfather Drosselmeier interrupted his story at this point, but promised to finish it on the following evening.

The Story of the Hard Nut, Concluded

❀

The very next evening, as soon as the lamps were lit, Godfather Drosselmeier returned and went on with his story:

Drosselmeier and the court astrologer traveled for fifteen years without finding any trace of the nut Krakatuk. I could go on month-by-month, describing precisely where they went and the amazing things they saw. But all those travels and wonders were of little comfort to Drosselmeier, who was becoming terribly discouraged and longed to see his beloved home town, Nuremberg, once more.

One day, as Drosselmeier and the court astrologer smoked their pipes in the middle of a great forest in Asia, Drosselmeier suddenly cried out:

❄

Oh, Nuremberg, Nuremberg, dear native place!

If a man doesn't know you, as he knows his own face—

Though far he has traveled, and great cities seen—

Such as London, and Paris, and Peterwardein—

He can't know what happiness really can be;

Still must his heart ever languish for thee!

For thee, Nuremberg, you exquisite town—

Where the houses have windows both upstairs and down!

❄

As Drosselmeier voiced this mournful lament, the astrologer began to weep so terribly that you could hear him from one side of Asia to the other. Finally he pulled himself together, wiped the tears from his eyes, and said, "My esteemed colleague, why should we sit here and howl? Why don't we go to Nuremberg? Haven't we as much chance of finding the elusive nut Krakatuk there as anywhere else?"

"That's true," answered Drosselmeier, feeling somewhat comforted. Right away they both stood up, knocked the ashes out of their pipes, and made a beeline straight from that forest in the center of Asia to Nuremberg.

They had just arrived when they paid a visit to Drosselmeier's

cousin, the dollmaker, Christoph Zacharias Drosselmeier, whom Drosselmeier hadn't seen in many many years. The clockmaker told his cousin the whole story of Princess Pirlipat, Dame Mouserinks, and the nut Krakatuk.

From time to time during the story, Christoph Zacharias would clap his hands and shout in amazement, "My goodness, you astonish me!"

Drosselmeier told him more about his long journey–how the Almond Prince had him banished in shame; how he'd asked in vain for help at the Squirreltown Natural History Association–in short, how he had been completely unsuccessful in uncovering a trace of the nut Krakatuk.

Finally Christoph Zacharias threw his cap and wig in the air, wrapped his arms around his cousin and cried, "Cousin, cousin, you've got it made–you really have it made–for unless I'm terribly mistaken, I have the nut Krakatuk myself!"

Wasting no time, he brought out a little cardboard box, from which he took a gilded nut of average size.

"There's an unusual story about this nut," he began. "A few years ago, a stranger showed up for Christmas with a sack of nuts to sell. Right in front of my toystore he got into an argument with the city nut sellers, and he put the sack down so that he could defend him-self. In a matter of seconds a wagon carrying a heavy load came along and drove over the sack. All the nuts were smashed except one, and the stranger suddenly offered to sell it to me if I could give him a silver twenty-crown piece from the year 1720 that hadn't lost its shine. This seemed strange to me. Stranger still, I found exactly the coin he wanted in my pocket. So I bought the nut and gilded it—though I couldn't ex-plain even to myself why I paid so much for the thing or took such trouble over it afterward."

Any doubt as to whether his cousin's nut was the long-sought Krakatuk vanished in a moment, when the court astrologer carefully scraped away the gilded gold and found the word *Krakatuk* engraved on the shell in Chinese characters.

Drosselmeier's joy was great. His cousin was happy as well, for Drosselmeier promised him that *he* too would benefit from the king's gratitude, which would include a good pension and all the gold leaf he would ever need for his gilding.

Late that evening, as the clockmaker and the astrologer had put on their nightcaps and were on their way to bed, the astrologer said, "My dear colleague, one bit of good luck never comes alone. Believe me, we've found not only the nut, but also the young man who will crack it and hand the kernel to the princess, making her beautiful

again. I mean none other than the son of your cousin! And I'm not

going to sleep," he added excitedly, "until I've drawn that youngster's

horoscope."

At once, he tore the nightcap from his head and rushed off to

consult the stars.

Cousin Christoph Zacharias's son was, in fact, a good-looking,

well-formed young man who hadn't yet shaved and never wore boots.

Over the course of many Christmas seasons, he had taken on the ap-

pearance of an elegant puppet, thanks to the pains his father took in

dressing him. His standard Christmas uniform consisted of a hand-

some red coat trimmed in gold, a sword, a hat under his arm, and an

elegant coiffure complete with pigtail. He would stand proudly in his

father's shop and, with natural gallantry, crack nuts for the young

ladies, who called him "the handsome nutcracker."

In the morning, the astrologer flung his arms around the

clockmaker, crying, "He's the one! Just two things, dear colleague, two

things that we must keep carefully in mind. First, we must construct an

extremely artful pigtail for this precious nephew of yours. It has to be

connected with his lower jaw in such a way that the pigtail can give

the jaw a very powerful pull. Second, when we get back to the palace we must conceal the fact that we have found the young man who will bite the nut. He must appear long after we do. There is a good reason for this delay. My horoscope has revealed that if two or three others bite at the nut first, without restoring the princess's lost beauty, the king will promise the man who does break it the princess's hand in marriage. He will also make him heir to the royal crown."

The dollmaker cousin was delighted at the thought that his son might marry Princess Pirlipat and become first a prince and then a king. The pigtail that Drosselmeier attached to his hopeful young nephew worked so well that the boy managed to crack the hardest of peach stones with the utmost ease.

With their preparations completed, Drosselmeier and the astrologer sent news to the palace that they had discovered the nut Krakatuk. The necessary advertisements were at once placed in the newspapers. By the time our travelers got back to the castle, there had already arrived several very handsome men, some of whom were princes, and all of whom believed that their healthy teeth had the power to break the curse hanging over the princess.

Our travelers were horrified when they saw poor Pirlipat again. The tiny body with its wispy hands and feet could barely hold the shapeless head up. The hideousness of the face was emphasized by a beard that grew like white cotton around the mouth and chin. No wonder her parents were so anxious to help her.

Everything came to pass exactly as the astrologer had predicted. One after another, the silly young men bit agonizingly into the nut without helping the princess in the slightest. As each unhappy contestant was carried out, nearly unconscious, by a team of dentists on hand, he would sigh, "That *was* a hard nut to crack."

When, with breaking heart, the king at last promised that whoever broke the enchantment would win both his daughter and his kingdom, the courtly young nephew Drosselmeier made his appearance and begged a chance to try.

None of the previous young men had pleased the princess so much. When she saw young Drosselmeier, she pressed her weak little hands to her heart and sighed, "Ah, may he be the one who can crack the nut and become my husband!"

When he had bowed to the king, the queen, and to Princess Pirlipat, young Drosselmeier received the nut Krakatuk from the hands of the Minister of Ceremonies. With no further ado, he placed it between his teeth, pulled hard on his pigtail, and–*k-nack–k-nack*–the shell

shattered into countless pieces. He then neatly cleaned away the pieces of husk that were sticking to the kernel and, with a polite flourish, he presented it to the princess. As soon as she took it, young Drosselmeier closed his eyes and began to walk backward.

The princess instantly swallowed the kernel, and–what joy it was to see!–the girl was transformed. There stood before the court an angelically beautiful girl with a face that seemed woven of delicate lily-white and rose-red silk, with eyes of sparkling azure, and hair like curling threads of gold.

The blare of trumpets and kettledrums mingled with the people's loud rejoicing. The king and his entire court danced around on one leg, as they had done at Pirlipat's birth, and the queen had to be revived with eau de Cologne, as she had fainted from joy and delight.

The uproar threw young Drosselmeier off balance–remember, he still had to finish taking his seven backward steps. But he controlled himself as best as he could, and he stretched his right foot back carefully to take his seventh step. Then–hideously peeping and squeaking–up came Dame Mouserinks through the floor. As young Drosselmeier put his foot down, he couldn't help stepping on her, and he stumbled and almost fell.

The horror of it! All at once the youth was transformed, just as the princess had been earlier: His body shriveled up until it could barely support his heavy shapeless head, which now had enormous popping eyes and a wide gaping mouth. Where his pigtail used to be, a scanty wooden cloak now hung down, controlling the movements of his lower jaw.

The clockmaker and the astrologer were wild with terror. As for Dame Mouserinks, she was scrabbling in her own blood on the floor. Her wickedness would not go unpunished, for young Drossel-meier had crushed her throat so deeply with the sharp point of his shoe that she was doomed to die.

As Dame Mouserinks lay in her death agony, she squeaked lamentably and cried,

❁

Oh, Krakatuk, you hard hard nut–

Because of you my life is shut!

Hee hee, fee fee, my nutcracking foe–

Soon you as well to death will go!

My little son with seven crowns

Will seek you out and pull you down.

He'll avenge his mother's death

With Nutcracker's dying breath!–

Oh, flowing blood, so hot and red,

In you I drown; you're my deathbed . . .

Queek~!

❈

With this cry, Dame Mouserinks died, and her body was car~
ried out by the court stovelighter.

As a result of this impassioned farewell by the evil witch, no
one had been paying much attention to young Drosselmeier. The
princess reminded the king of his promise, and so it happened that the
young man was brought into the royal presence again. But when he
came forward in his wretched, transformed condition, the princess put
both her hands to her face and cried, "Somebody take away that awful
little Nutcracker!"

The Lord Chamberlain at once seized him by his little shoul~
ders and threw him out the door. The king was furious that anyone
would suggest that he take a Nutcracker as a son~in~law. Naturally, he
laid all the blame upon the clockmaker and the astrologer and he ban~
ished them both from the palace forever.

The horoscope hadn't predicted this turn of events. However,
that did not prevent the astrologer from studying the stars once more

and making some fresh observations. The stars told him that young Drosselmeier would acquit himself so well in his new condition that he would still become a prince and a king, in spite of his transformation. He also learned that Drosselmeier's deformity would disappear only when two conditions were met. First, Dame Mouserinks's son—the seven-headed King of Mice, born after her original seven sons had died—would have to meet his own death at the Nutcracker's hand. Second, a lady would have to fall in love with him despite his ugliness.

That, my dear children, said Godfather Drosselmeier, is the story of the hard nut. Now you know why people so often use the expression, "That was a hard nut to crack," and why nutcrackers are so ugly.

Thus did Godfather Drosselmeier finish his long tale. Marie thought Princess Pirlipat was a vile and ungrateful thing. Fritz, however, felt that if Nutcracker really were the right kind of fellow, he would soon bring the Mouse King into line and win back his good looks.

Uncle  Nephew

If any of my readers has ever had the misfortune to cut themselves on glass, they will know how much it hurts and how awful long it takes to heal. Marie had to stay in bed a whole week, because she felt dizzy as soon as she tried to stand up. But at last she was well again, and able to run around the house as before.

In the glass cabinet, everything looked in order—trees and flowers and houses, dolls and toys, everything new and shiny. Most important, Marie found her dear Nutcracker there again. He stood on the second shelf, smiling at her with completely healed teeth.

Marie suddenly knew that her Nutcracker was none other than young Mr. Drosselmeier of Nuremberg—Godfather Drosselmeier's courtly nephew—who was still under the curse of Dame Mouserinks. As for the clever clockmaker in the court of Pirlipat's father the king, it had to be Godfather Drosselmeier himself.

"Why didn't your uncle help you?" Marie cried sorrowfully. She became more and more convinced each moment that the battle she had watched had been fought over nothing less than Nutcracker's right to the crown and kingdom. Weren't all the other toys rightfully

his subjects? And wasn't it clear that the astrologer's prophecy had

come true, that Nutcracker was the rightful king of Toyland?

While the clever Marie was weighing all these questions in her

mind, she kept expecting Nutcracker and his followers to give some in-

dication of being alive. This, however, did not come to pass. Everything

in the cabinet remained quite motionless. Marie attributed this to the

effect of the evil curses wrought by Dame Mouserinks and her seven-

headed son, the Mouse King.

"But," Marie whispered, "though you're not able to move or

even to say the least little word to me, dear young Drosselmeier, I know

you understand that I want only the best for you. You can always count

on my assistance when you need it. And I am going to ask your uncle,

Godfather Drosselmeier, to muster all his skill to help you as well."

Nutcracker remained motionless. It seemed to Marie, however,

that a gentle sigh was audible through the glass cabinet. The sigh made

the panes ring with a faint but enchanting music. Then she heard a

sound like a little bell singing, "Marie so fine~oh, angel mine! I will be

thine, if thou wilt be mine!"

This little song made Marie shiver. It also gave her great

pleasure. ·

As twilight crept in, Marie's father arrived with Godfather Drosselmeier. Soon Louise set out the tea table and the family seated themselves around it, discussing pleasant subjects. Marie pulled up her little stool and sat at her godfather's feet in silence.

During a brief lull in the conversation, Marie looked Godfather Drosselmeier full in the face with her great blue eyes and said, "I know now, Godfather, that my Nutcracker is your nephew, young Mr. Drosselmeier from Nuremberg. The prophecy has come true: He is a king and a prince, just as your friend the astrologer said he would be. But you know as well as I do that he is at war with Dame Mouserinks's son—that awful King of the Mice. Why don't you help him?"

Marie now told her entire family the story of the battle as she had witnessed it. She was frequently interrupted by the loud laughter of her father, mother and sister. But Fritz and Godfather Drosselmeier listened quite gravely.

"How in the world did that child stuff all that nonsense into her head?" exclaimed her father.

"She has a lively imagination, that's all," said her mother. "This is just a dream that came from the wound fever in her arm."

"It *must* be nonsense," Fritz asserted. "My red soldiers are not cowards. If they were, do you think I'd be their commander?"

Godfather smiled strangely and took little Marie on his knee, speaking more gently to her than ever he'd been known to do before.

"Oh, my little Marie," he said. "You have been singled out more than any of the rest of us. You are a born princess, like Pirlipat, and you reign over a bright and beautiful country. But you still have much to suffer if you want to help your poor deformed Nutcracker, for the King of Mice nips at his heels with every step. I cannot help him. You, and you alone, can do that. So be faithful and true."

Neither Marie nor any of the others knew what Godfather Drosselmeier meant by these words. They struck Dr. Stahlbaum—Marie's father—as being so strange that he felt Drosselmeier's pulse and said, "There seems to be quite a bit of congestion of blood in your head, my dear sir. I'll write you a prescription."

But Marie's mother shook her head thoughtfully and said, "I think I know what Godfather Drosselmeier means, though I can't exactly put it into words."

Victory

Not long afterwards,   Marie was awakened one bright moonlit night by a strange noise

coming from a corner of her room. It sounded as if a number of small stones were being thrown here and

there. There was also a horrible cheeping and squeaking.

"Oh no! The mice—the mice are coming back again!" Marie

cried, terrified. She wanted to wake her mother. But suddenly the

noises died away—and Marie felt frozen beneath her covers, unable to

move a muscle. Just then she saw the King of Mice emerging through

a hole in the wall, gazing about with his glittering beady eyes. His

seven crowns were gleaming. At last, he entered the room and skittered

about triumphantly, coming to a halt on the little table at the head of

her bed.

"Hee-hee-hee! Now you have to give me your candy, your cakes,

your marzipan—all your tasty little treats! If you don't, you may watch

while I gnaw on your precious Nutcracker!"

Thus piped the Mouse King, hideously grinding and chattering his teeth—and then, just as suddenly, he jumped back through the hole

in the wall and disappeared.

Marie was so terrified by this threat that in the morning she

was quite pale and could barely utter a word. A hundred times she

wanted to tell her mother or her sister, or at least Fritz, what had hap-

pened. She stopped herself, thinking, *Of course, none of them would*

believe me—and do I really want to be laughed at?

It was clear to her that in order to help Nutcracker she would

have to sacrifice all her sweets. So that evening, she spread them out at

the bottom of the cabinet.

The next morning her mother said, "I can't figure out how

mice have suddenly gotten into the sitting-room. Just look, Marie,

they've eaten up all your candy."

Not quite all the candy had been eaten. The Mouse King, who

fancied himself a gourmet, hadn't found the marzipan quite to his

taste. His sharp little teeth had gnawed it all around the edges, so what

was left still had to be thrown away.

Marie did not mind losing her candy. She was overjoyed to

think that she had saved Nutcracker by giving it up. But imagine her

despair when, that night, she again heard a squeaking and peeping in her ear. Alas! Mouse King had appeared once more, and his eyes were glittering even more hatefully than the night before.

Now he commanded Marie, "Give me your sugar dolls, you nasty little thing, or I'm going to chew up *your* Nutcracker!"

With that, the horrid gray Mouse King sprang away and disappeared again.

Marie was disheartened. The next morning she went to the glass cabinet and looked mournfully at her sugar dolls. Dear readers, please believe that the most enchanting, artful little figures ever formed out of sugar paste belonged to Marie Stahlbaum. She had a very handsome little shepherd and shepherdess tending a flock of milk-white lambs, with a lively little dog jumping about them. There were also two postmen with letters in their hands, as well as four couples consisting of very well-dressed young gentlemen and ladies, all perched on a Russian seesaw. In addition, there were graceful dancers, a farmer with eyes fashioned from caraway seeds and a brave Joan of Arc with sugar-glazed armor. Back in the corner, however, there was a rosy-cheeked little baby, and this was Marie's darling. Tears came to her eyes.

"Oh, dear young Mr. Drosselmeier!" she cried as she turned to

Nutcracker, "there's really nothing I wouldn't do to help you—but this is very hard."

Nutcracker looked at her so pitifully that Marie could almost see the Mouse King's seven ugly mouths opening wide to swallow the poor young man. So that night she laid all her sugar dolls out in front of the cabinet, as she had done with the candy the night before. She kissed the shepherd, the shepherdess, and the lambs. At the very last, she brought out the little rosy-cheeked baby—and she did put it well in the back of the rest. The caraway seed farmer and Joan of Arc were made to stand guard in the first row.

"This is really getting to be a problem," Marie's mother said the next morning. "A huge and very hungry mouse must be living in the glass cabinet, for all Marie's nice little sugar figures have been nibbled and half-eaten." Marie, who had come downstairs and seen the dreadful damage, could not hold back her tears. Soon, however, she was able to smile again, for she thought, *What does it matter, as long as Nutcracker is safe?*

In the evening, Marie's mother told Dr. Stahlbaum and Godfather Drosselmeier about the havoc some mouse was wreaking in the glass cabinet. "What a nuisance!" her father declared emphatically.

"I have a solution!" Fritz broke in. "The baker down the street has a gray cat with a fine straight tail. I'll go and get hold of him. He'll take charge of the situation and bite the mouse's head off—even if it's Dame Mouserinks herself, or her son, the King of the Mice."

"Oh yes!" said his mother, smiling ruefully. "And then he'll jump up on the chairs and tables, knock down the cups and glasses, and ruin a thousand other things besides."

"No, no!" answered Fritz. "The baker's cat is beautifully trained. I wish I could maneuver on the edge of the roof the way he does."

"We can't have a cat in the house at night," said Louise, who hated cats.

"Fritz might be right about trying out a cat," Mama said at last. "Unless we could set a mousetrap instead. Do we have one?"

"Godfather Drosselmeier can make one for us," said Fritz. "He's the one who invented them, you know."

Everybody laughed. When Mama checked, she found they didn't have a trap in the house. But Godfather Drosselmeier said that he had quite a lot of them, and within the hour he had an excellent mousetrap sent over.

Godfather Drosselmeier's story of the hard nut was still very much on Marie's mind. While the Stahlbaums' cook was browning

some fat to use as bait for the traps, Marie shivered and blurted out,

"Oh, protect yourself from Dame Mouserinks and her family!"

Fritz took out his sword and said, "No, just let them come—I'll

take care of them!"

As night set in, Godfather Drosselmeier strung the bits of fat

on a fine thread and set the trap gently, gently in the glass cabinet. Fritz

warned, "Watch out, Godfather, and make sure the Mouse King doesn't

play a trick on you!"

How did it go for poor Marie that night? Something as cold as

ice went skittering over and around her arm, and then something

rough and horrible laid itself on her cheek and cheeped and squeaked in

her ear. The evil Mouse King settled, finally, on her shoulder, oozing a

blood red foam from all seven of his mouths. With a chattering and

grinding of his teeth, he hissed into Marie's ear,

❀

Sss, sss, I stay away from the feast—

It's meant to attack the hungriest beast—

A trap! A trap! I won't be caught!

Sss . . . Now, little girl, you must give me your books,

And your pretty new dress with its buttons and hooks.

Do all that I say, just as you ought.

For if you refuse, Nutcracker you'll lose!

I'll bite him and chew him, and show him hard use.

Hee-hee–peep-peep–squeak!

❀

Marie was overwhelmed with grief. She turned pale the next morning when her mother told her, "That disgusting mouse hasn't been caught." Mama thought that Marie was worried about what else the mouse would do to her fancy dolls and tried to reassure her: "Don't you worry, dear, we'll catch the nasty thing yet. If the traps don't help, Fritz will borrow the baker's cat."

As soon as Marie was alone in the sitting room, she went to the glass cabinet and sobbed to Nutcracker, "Oh, my dear, good Mr. Drosselmeier, what can a poor, unlucky little girl do for you? Even if I give that awful King of Mice all of my picture books to chew on, and the beautiful new dress that the Christ Child gave me at Christmas too, he's sure to go on asking for more. Soon I won't have anything left, and he'll want to eat *me!* Oh, what can I do? What can I do?"

As she went on crying, Marie noticed that there was a spot of blood left on Nutcracker's neck from the night of the battle. Ever since she had realized that Nutcracker was really young Mr. Drosselmeier, her godfather's nephew, she'd stopped carrying him in her arms and petting and kissing him. Indeed, she felt hesitant about touching him at all, for fear of seeming disrespectful. But now she took him carefully off of his shelf and wiped the blood away with her handkerchief.

Imagine how she felt when she found that Nutcracker was growing warmer and warmer in her hand, and beginning to move!

She put him back on his shelf as fast as she could. His mouth began to wobble back and forth, and he managed, with great difficulty, to say, "Ah, dearest Mademoiselle Stahlbaum, most precious of friends, how can I ever thank you for all you've done? No, don't sacrifice any of your picture books or your pretty new dress for me. Just get me a sword–yes, a sword. If you get me that, I'll take care of the rest . . . even . . . though . . . he . . ."

As Nutcracker's speech died away, his eyes, which had been filled with sympathy, grew lifeless again.

Marie felt an intense joy, now that she knew a way to help Nutcracker without having to make any more painful sacrifices. But where on earth could she get hold of a sword?

She decided to consult Fritz. That evening, when their father and mother had gone out and the two children were sitting beside the glass cabinet, she told him what had passed between her and Nut-cracker and the Mouse King, and asked him to provide the needed sword.

This time her account was so convincing that Fritz truly began to believe it. What concerned him most, at first, was Marie's descrip-tion of the shameful way his soldiers had behaved in the great battle. He asked her once more, very seriously, if they really had been so cow-ardly. When she gave him her word, Fritz went straight to the cabinet, gave his soldiers a most moving speech, and as punishment for their ab-ject retreat, solemnly plucked the soldiers' plumes out of their caps one by one and forbade the buglers to sound the march for a whole year.

When he had completed this sorrowful duty, he turned to Marie and said, "As far as the sword is concerned, I believe I can help Nutcracker. I placed an old colonel of the swordsmen on retirement with a pension yesterday, so he won't be needing his saber, which is very sharp."

This colonel had been settled, with his pension, in the back cor-ner of the third shelf. Fritz brought him out and removed his saber, which was still bright and fashioned from shining silver, and buckled it around the waist of Nutcracker.

That night Marie was so anxious she couldn't sleep. Around midnight she thought she heard strange noises in the sitting-room—rustling and clanging—and then suddenly there came a shrill *Queek!*

"The Mouse King! The Mouse King!" she cried, and jumped out of bed in terror.

Everything was silent. But soon there came a gentle tapping at the door of her room, and a soft voice said, "Don't be afraid, dearest Mademoiselle Stahlbaum! I have good news!"

Marie recognized young Drosselmeier's voice. She threw on her robe and flung open the door.

There stood Nutcracker, with his sword, now bloody, in his right hand, and a little wax candle in his left. When he saw Marie, he sank down on one knee and said, "It was you, and only you, dearest lady, who inspired me with knightly courage. You gave my arm the strength to fight the rogue who dared insult you. Now the wicked King of Mice lies wounded and writhing in his own blood! Please consent, dear lady, to accept these tokens of victory from the hand of the one who is, until death, your true and faithful knight."

Nutcracker took the seven golden crowns of the Mouse King

from his left arm, upon which he had them ringed in sequence. He

handed them to Marie, who accepted them with joy.

Nutcracker rose and continued, "Oh, my dearly beloved Made-

moiselle Stahlbaum, now that I have finally defeated my longtime

enemy, I can show you such wonderful things! If you would just be so

good as to follow me for a few steps. Oh, do come with me, dearest

lady!"

Toyland

I'm sure none of you would have hesitated for a moment to go with the good Nutcracker, who had

always shown himself to have such a golden  heart. Marie did it all the more willingly because

she knew she had a right to his gratitude.

"I will go with you, dear Mr. Drosselmeier," Marie assured him.

"But we can't go very far, and we can't be away very long–because, you

know, I still haven't had any sleep yet."

"Then we'll go by the shortest route," said Nutcracker. "Al-

though it is also the most difficult."

He began to march across the floor, and Marie followed until

he stopped in front of a big old wardrobe. Marie was surprised to see

that, although the doors of this wardrobe were usually shut, they were

now wide open. She could see her father's traveling cloak of fox fur

hanging in the front.

Nutcracker climbed deftly up this cloak, clinging to the edging,

and seized hold of the long tassel that fastened the back of it. He gave

this tassel a tug, and a pretty ladder of cedarwood fell quickly down through one of the armholes of the cloak.

"Miss Stahlbaum, step up on that ladder, if you will be so kind," said Nutcracker.

Marie did so. As soon as she had climbed up through the arm-hole and began to look out at the neck, a dazzling light came pouring over her—and she found herself standing on a lovely, sweet-scented meadow that sparkled as if it were flowering with rich gems.

"We are now in Candy Meadow," said Nutcracker, "Next we will pass through that gate over there."

Marie looked up and saw a beautiful gateway on the meadow, only a few steps away. It seemed to be made of white, brown, and purple-colored marble. But when she came closer she saw it was made of baked sugar almonds and raisins, which—as Nutcracker said as they were going through it—was the reason it was called the Almond and Raisin Gate. On a gallery above, made of barley sugar, six monkeys dressed in red doublets were playing rousing music on brass instru-ments.

Marie observed that she was walking along on what seemed to be a multicolored marble pavement—which, however, was really a mosaic of hard candies. Presently the sweetest of odors—like that of an orange grove in full bloom—came wafting about her, emanating from a little forest that bordered both sides of the path. There was such a glitter and sparkle lighting up the dark foliage that she could see gold and silver fruits hanging on the multi-tinted branches of the trees. These branches were all decorated with ribbons and bunches of flowers, like members of a wedding party. The gold-leaf and silver-tinsel fruits and foliage rustled and tinkled like beautiful music, to which the sparkling lights could not help dancing.

"How wonderful this is!" cried Marie, enraptured.

"This is Christmas Forest, dear mademoiselle," said Nutcracker.

"Ah," said Marie, "if I could only stay here a little while!"

Nutcracker clapped his hands, and immediately there arrived a troupe of shepherds and shepherdesses, as well as hunters and huntresses, all of whom were so white and delicate that you would have thought they were made of pure sugar. Marie had glimpsed them before, while they were walking about in the trees. They produced a fine gold reclining chair, laid a white satin cushion upon it, and courteously invited Marie to take a seat. As soon as she did so, the shepherds and shepherdesses performed a pretty ballet before her, while the hunters and huntresses played music on their horns.

All of a sudden, as if by a signal, they disappeared into the undergrowth.

"Please forgive me for the poor style in which this dance was executed, dearest Mademoiselle Stahlbaum," said Nutcracker. "These people all belong to our Wire Ballet Company, and they can only repeat the same motions over and over again. Shouldn't we walk on a little farther?"

"Oh, it was really all very beautiful, and I'm terribly pleased with everything!" said Marie, as she stood up and followed Nutcracker.

They walked by the side of a gently rippling brook, which seemed to be the source of the delicate scent that filled the forest.

"This is Orangewater Brook," said Nutcracker. "Except for its sweet scent, it is nowhere as fine as the Lemonade River, a beautiful broad stream that flows—just like this one—into the Almond-Milk Sea."

Marie soon heard a louder splashing and rushing, and saw the Lemonade River itself, which went rolling along in waves of a pale yellow, between banks covered with grass that shone like green jewels. A remarkable freshness and coolness, strengthening the heart and spirit, exhaled from this fine river.

Not far off, a dark yellow stream crept sluggishly along, giving out another delicious aroma. On its banks, a number of pretty children sat angling for fat fish that they ate as soon as they caught them. These fish were shaped like hazelnuts, as Marie saw when she came closer.

A short distance farther along the banks of this smaller, slower stream stood a nice village. The church, the parsonage, the barns, and the houses, were all dark brown with gilt roofs. Many of the walls looked as if they were plastered over with lemon peel and shelled almonds.

"This village is Gingerthorpe-on-the-Honey," said Nutcracker. "It's famous for the good looks of its inhabitants. But they are very short-tempered people, because they suffer so much from toothache. We won't go there at present."

Just then, Marie caught sight of another small town where the houses were fashioned in all sorts of lovely colors. Nutcracker led the way into this town. Marie heard sounds of bustle and merriment, and soon she saw thousands of little people unloading a multitude of wagons that had been drawn up in the marketplace. What they were

unloading looked like packages of colored paper and blocks of chocolate.

"This is Bonbonville," Nutcracker said. "A diplomatic corps has

just arrived jointly from Paperland and the King of Chocolate. These

poor people of Bonbonville have lately been threatened by the Fly Ad-

miral's forces, so they are using the colored wrapping supplied by

Paperland to protect their houses. And they are also building fortifica-

tions with the fine blocks that the Chocolate King has sent them. But,

dearest mademoiselle, enough of these small towns! Let's be off to the

capital."

He moved quickly onward, and Marie followed him, full of

anticipation. Soon a rosy vapor appeared, suffusing everything with a

soft splendor. She saw that this mist was the reflection from a huge,

shining rose-red body of water, which rippled before them in pinkish

wavelets. Upon this delightful water, lovely swans were floating, white

and silver, with collars of gold. As if competing with each other, the

swans sang in turn, each song more beautiful than the last. In time to

this music, schools of fish swirled in the rosy ripples, glittering like

diamonds.

"Oh!" cried Marie, extremely excited. "This must be the lake that Godfather Drosselmeier was going to make for me, and I must be

the girl who gets to play with the swans."

Nutcracker laughed in a scornful manner that Marie had

never heard from him before. He said, "My uncle could never make

something like this. You yourself would have a better chance of accom-

plishing such a feat. But never mind . . . Why don't we go sailing over

Lake Rosa to our capital city?"

the Capital

Nutcracker clapped his little hands again,  and the waves of Lake Rosa began to sound

louder and to splash higher. Marie saw that a shell-shaped chariot of the waves, built from multicolored flashing

gemstones, was approaching from the distance, drawn by two dolphins with skins of gold. Twelve dark little

boys jumped to the land, all of them wearing headdresses and doublets

made of hummingbirds' feathers woven together. Their feet glid-

ing gently along the water's surface, they carried first Marie and

then Nutcracker into the chariot, which immediately began to cross

the lake.

Oh, it was lovely for Marie, gliding over the waters in that

shell-shaped chariot, with rosy perfume filling her nostrils and pink

waves lapping lightly at the boat. The two golden-skinned dolphins

cleared their blowholes and sent crystalline fountains high in the air.

These formed gleaming rainbows as they fell. As these dolphins swam

together they sang in fine silvery voices:

✵

Who glides upon the lake so rosy?

A fairy! Sing, wavelets, *Bim-bim;*

Little fishes, *Sim-sim;*

Little swans, *Shwah-shwah;*

Golden birds, *Tra-rah!*

Waves and tide, you'd best get busy—

Tinkle and tap and mutter;

Ripple and swell and flutter!

For a fairy on you now reposes,

Lying on a billow of roses—

So whirl and whush and rush—

Bring her to us! To us!

✵

The twelve little boys who now stood at the back of the
chariot seemed offended by this song. They shook the long palm
leaves that they were holding so that the fronds clattered and rattled together. Then they stamped their feet to a new rhythm and
sang:

❁

Klapp and *klipp,* and *klipp* and *klapp–*

Up and back!

Our voices won't be drowned!

So flee, little fishes; and flee, slender swans,

Our shell-boat's bearing down!

Klapp and *klipp,* and *klipp* and *klapp–*

Up and back!

❁

"Those boys are quite amusing fellows," Nutcracker conceded,

though he was obviously a bit annoyed. "But you see that they have a

way of getting the whole lake in an uproar."

Both water and air were now churning with the deafening din

of otherwordly voices. Marie went on gazing into the rosy perfumed

waves, on each wave a pretty girl's face smiled back at her.

"Oh, look at Princess Pirlipat," she cried, clapping her hands

with joy. "Just look at her, dear Mr. Drosselmeier! There's Princess Pir-

lipat, under the water, smiling at me so sweetly."

Nutcracker sighed sorrowfully. "My dearest Mademoiselle

Stahlbaum, that isn't Princess Pirlipat. It is you, and always you, whom

you see smiling up from those rosy waves."

Marie pulled her head back quickly, closed her eyes as tightly as she could, and felt extremely embarrassed. At that very moment, the twelve little boys lifted her out of the chariot and set her on shore. She found herself in a small thicket that was nearly as beautiful as Christmas Forest—so much did everything glitter and sparkle in it. The fruit on the trees amazed her, not just because of its unusual colors, but also because of its delicious perfume.

"Ah," said Nutcracker, "here we are in Jelly-and-Jam Grove. You see, over there lies the capital."

How can I begin, dear children, to describe the beauty and richness of the city that unfolded before Marie as she crossed a flowery plain? Not only were there walls and towers shining in gorgeous colors, but the very shapes of the buildings were like nothing ever seen before on earth. Instead of roofs, the houses were topped with jeweled crowns, while the towers were finely sculpted and patterned with intertwined leaves.

As Marie and Nutcracker passed through the gateway—which was made of macaroons and sugared fruits—a troop of silver soldiers saluted them. Then a small man in a brocade robe threw his arms around Nutcracker's neck, crying, "Welcome, dearest prince! Welcome to Sweettown!"

Marie was more than a little surprised to hear such an elegant person address young Mr. Drosselmeier as a prince. But she was soon distracted by a swirl of small delicate voices talking around her. There was so much laughing and chattering, and singing and playing of instruments, that Marie could pay attention to nothing else. She asked Nutcracker what it all meant.

"Oh, it's not unusual, dearest Mademoiselle Stahlbaum," he answered. "Sweettown is a well-populated, happy city, and what you see now goes on here every day. Please come along a little farther."

With just a few more steps they came to the great marketplace, which was utterly magnificent. The houses surrounding the square were made of filagreed sugarwork, with balconies perched above balconies. In the center of the square, there stood, like an obelisk, a lofty cake covered with sugar. The fountains around this cake spouted almond soda, lemonade, and other sweet drinks into the air. The gutters around the square were full of cream, which the people spooned up whenever they pleased.

Thronging through the square were delightful small people numbering in the thousands, shouting, laughing, playing and singing—in short, making all that joyful noise that Marie had already heard from a distance. There were beautifully dressed ladies and gentlemen, Greeks and Nubians, Tyrolese and Chinese, officers and soldiers, clergymen,

shepherds, roly-poly sausage-men. Every conceivable type of person

was parading about.

The tumult grew louder in one of the corners. The people there

were clearing a path. For the Great Mogul happened to be passing along

in his canopied palanquin, attended by ninety-three grandees of the

realm and seven hundred servants. It so happened that the Fisherman's

Guild, about five hundred strong, were celebrating a festival in the op-

posite corner of the square. What an unfortunate coincidence that the

Grand Turk also chose this moment to cross the square with three

thousand janissaries, just as the fishermen were marching up to the

cake obelisk singing, "Hail! All hail to the glorious sun!"

The result was a thronging and shoving, shouting and squeak-

ing. Soon lamentations arose, as did wails of pain, for one of the fisher-

men had knocked off a Brahmin's head, while the Great Mogul had

been very nearly run down by a sausage-man. The din grew wilder

and wilder. Fist fights were beginning to break out when the man in

the brocade robe who had called Nutcracker a prince climbed up to the

top of the cake obelisk. After a bell had rung very clearly three times,

this man shouted, "Pastrycook! Pastrycook! Pastrycook!"

Instantly the chaos subsided. After the entangled processions had been disentangled, the dirt properly brushed off the Great Mogul,

and the Brahmin's head stuck on once more, the merry noise began

again.

"Why did that gentleman call out 'Pastrycook,' Mr. Drossel-

meier?" Marie asked.

"Ah, dear Mademoiselle Stahlbaum," said Nutcracker, "in this

place 'Pastrycook' means a mysterious and terrible power that repre-

sents the Fate or Destiny that rules these happy people. They're so

afraid of it that simply saying its name will end the wildest tumult in

a moment, as the mayor has just demonstrated. When they hear that

name, nobody thinks any more about earthly insults—punches in the

ribs, broken heads, and so on. Everyone looks inward and asks, 'What

does it mean to be human?' and 'What can I do with my humanity?' "

Suddenly Marie found herself standing in front of an astonish-

ing castle that glowed pink and was ornamented with a hundred beau-

tiful towers. Here and there upon its walls rich bouquets of violets,

narcissuses, tulips, and carnations were blooming. Their dark, glowing

colors heightened the dazzling rose-tinged whiteness of the walls. The

great dome of the central building, as well as the pyramid-shaped roofs

of the towers, were studded with thousands of sparkling gold and sil-

ver stars.

"Voilà," said Nutcracker, "here we are at Marzipan Castle."

Marie noticed that one of the biggest towers was missing a roof, and that some men up on a scaffold made of cinnamon sticks were busy putting it on again.

Nutcracker saw her questioning look and said, "This beautiful castle was threatened a short time ago with serious damage, if not with total destruction. Sweet-Tooth the giant happened to be passing by, and he bit off the top of that tower and began to gnaw at the great dome. To placate him, the Sweettown people brought him an entire quarter of the city, and threw in a considerable slice of Jelly-and-Jam Grove as well. That finally filled up Sweet-Tooth, and he went on his way."

Now Marie heard soft, beautiful music playing. Out came twelve pages with lighted clove sticks which they held in their hands like torches. Their heads were made of pearls, their bodies were fash-ioned from emeralds and rubies, and their feet were beautifully worked pure gold. After them came four ladies about the size of Marie's Miss Klara, but so gloriously and brilliantly attired that Marie knew them to be princesses born and bred. They embraced Nutcracker most tenderly and shed tears of gladness, saying, "Oh, prince—dearest prince! Beloved brother!"

Nutcracker seemed deeply touched. He wiped tears from his eyes, for they were flowing thick and fast. Then he took Marie by the hand and said, "This is Mademoiselle Marie Stahlbaum, the daughter of a highly respectable doctor. She is the one who saved my life! If she hadn't thrown her slipper just in the nick of time—and if she hadn't obtained the retired colonel's sword for me—I would be lying in a cold grave at this moment, bitten to death by the evil Mouse King. I ask all of you here today, do you think that Pirlipat—princess though she is—can compare for a moment to Mademoiselle Stahlbaum in beauty, in goodness, or in virtue of any kind? I say, No! No!"

All of the ladies cried "No" as well. They embraced Marie and praised her in unison: "Oh, you noble savior of our beloved princely brother—excellent Mademoiselle Stahlbaum!"

Now they led Marie and Nutcracker into a hall of the castle where the walls were constructed of sparkling crystal. Marie was delighted by the furniture. There were the loveliest chairs, bureaus, and dining tables, all made of cedar or brazilwood, and all covered with golden flowers.

The princesses bade Marie and Nutcracker sit down, and then went off to prepare a banquet. Soon they returned with vast quantities of cups and dishes of the finest Japanese porcelain, as well as spoons,

knives and forks, graters and stew pans, and other kitchen utensils of

gold and silver. They also fetched the most delightful fruits and began

to squeeze them daintily in their white hands and to mingle them with

grated spices and sugared almonds. Marie could see how gifted these

princesses were in the culinary arts and knew that she was in store for

a magnificent banquet. But Marie also excelled at cookery and she

secretly wished that she could help the princesses.

As if she had read Marie's mind, the prettiest of Nutcracker's

sisters handed her a little gold mortar and said, "Sweet friend, dear res-

cuer of my brother, would you mind grinding up a bit of this sugar?"

Marie ground the mortar willingly. The sound of the scraping

was like a lovely song. As she worked, Nutcracker described in detail

the battle between his army and that of the Mouse King–how his

troops had behaved so badly, how the horrible Mouse King had all but

bitten him to death, and how Marie had willingly sacrificed her most

precious candies and toys to save him.

During all this it seemed to Marie as if what Nutcracker was

saying–and even the grating sound of her mortar–was growing ever

more indistinct. Presently she became aware that a silver mist was forming around her like a cloud. The princesses, the pages, Nutcracker,

and Marie herself were floating within it. A strange singing and

buzzing and humming arose, then died away in the distance . . . Marie

felt as if she were riding the crest of a wave, climbing higher and

higher—higher and higher—higher and . . .

———◆•※•◆———

Conclusion

Pum-poof! Marie fell from an unimagin- able height. My, what a crash! When

she opened her eyes, she was lying in her own bed! It was broad daylight, and her mother was standing

before her, saying, "Well, what a sleep you have had! Breakfast has been ready for a long time now."

Of course, dear reader, you understand what happened, don't

you? Marie, confounded and amazed by all the wonderful things she

had seen, had finally drifted off to sleep in Marzipan Castle, and the

chariot boys, or the pages, or perhaps the princesses themselves, had

carried her home and put her to bed.

"Oh, Mama darling," said Marie, "you'd be surprised to hear

where young Mr. Drosselmeier took me during the night, and what

beautiful things I have seen!" And she told her mother the same faith-

ful account as I have told you.

Mama listened with astonishment. When Marie had finished,

she said to her lovely daughter, "You have had a long, beautiful dream,

Marie. But now you must put it all out of your head."

Marie insisted that she hadn't been dreaming at all. So her mother took her to the glass cabinet in the sitting-room, lifted out Nutcracker from his usual position on the third shelf, and said, "You silly girl, how can you believe that this wooden figure can live and move around on its own?" The whole family waited for her reply.

"Oh, Mama," answered Marie, "I know perfectly well that Nutcracker is young Mr. Drosselmeier from Nuremberg, Godfather Drosselmeier's nephew."

Her mother and father both burst out laughing.

Marie nearly broke into tears. "Oh, Father! Now *you're* laughing at my poor Nutcracker too!" she cried. "I'll have you know he spoke very highly of *you*. When we arrived at Marzipan Castle and he was introducing me to his sisters, the princesses, he said that you were 'a highly respectable medical man.' "

The laughter grew louder. Louise and even Fritz joined in. Marie ran into the next room, took the Mouse King's seven crowns from her box, then returned and handed them to her mother, saying, "Look here, then, Mama. These are the Mouse King's seven crowns, which young Mr. Drosselmeier gave me last night as proof that he had won the battle."

Her mother gazed in amazement at the tiny crowns, which were made of some very shiny metal she'd never seen before, and had been worked more beautifully that any human hands could have worked them. Dr. Stahlbaum could not stop looking at the crowns either, and both of her parents begged Marie to tell them where she really had gotten them.

She could only repeat what she had said before. When her father scolded her and accused her of lying, she began to cry bitterly and said, "Can't you believe your own daughter?"

At this moment, the door opened and Godfather Drosselmeier came in, calling, "Hello! Hello! What's going on? Why is my little Marie crying?"

Dr. Stahlbaum told him the whole story and showed him the crowns. Drosselmeier barely had to look at them before he declared, "Stuff and nonsense! These are the crowns I used to wear on my watch chain. I gave them as a present to Marie on her second birthday. Don't you remember?"

Dr. and Mrs. Stahlbaum couldn't actually remember. But Marie, seeing that her father's and mother's faces had relaxed again, ran up to Drosselmeier and cried, "You understand everything, Godfather.

Now explain it to them. Let them hear from your own lips that my Nutcracker is your nephew, young Mr. Drosselmeier of Nuremberg, and that he's the one who gave me the crowns."

Drosselmeier made a very angry face and muttered, "Oh, that's pure nonsense!"

Marie's father set her down in front of him and said, "Now listen, Marie. Let's put an end to all this storytelling once and for all. I'm not going to allow any more of it, and if ever I hear you saying again that this idiotic, ugly Nutcracker is your godfather's nephew, I'll throw him out the window—and not just him, but all your other playthings too, even Miss Klara."

Of course, after that, poor Marie didn't dare say another word about the one subject that occupied her entire mind—though I'm sure, dear reader, that you realize how impossible it would be for anyone who had seen all that Marie had seen to forget it.

I regret to say that even Fritz turned his back on his sister when she wanted to talk to him about the wondrous land in which she'd been so happy. In fact, he would grind his teeth and mutter, "Silly girl!"—rather a mean thing for an otherwise kind brother to say to his sister.

Since Fritz no longer believed what his sister had said, he ordered a public parade and formally withdrew the reprimand he had given his soldiers. To replace the plumes he had taken from them, he gave them much taller and finer ones of goose feathers.

Marie was left with no other choice but to keep her adventures to herself. But images of the enchanting fairy realm lingered in her mind, and the music of that delightful, happy country still rang deliciously in her ears. Whenever she recalled those wonders, she experienced them again. As a result, she often sat quiet and meditative, absorbed within herself. Everybody scolded her for being such a dreamer.

Then, one day, it so happened that Godfather Drosselmeier was repairing one of the clocks in the house while Marie was sitting by the glass cabinet, lost in her dreams, gazing at Nutcracker. All at once she said aloud, despite herself, "Ah, dear Mr. Drosselmeier, if only you really were alive! I wouldn't act like Princess Pirlipat—I'd never reject you, no matter how ugly you got!"

"Hrumph! What nonsense!" said Godfather Drosselmeier.

As he spoke, there came such a tremendous rumble and bang that Marie was knocked out of her chair unconscious.

When she came back to her senses, her mother was bustling around her. "How could you fall off your chair like that, a big girl like you?" Mama asked her, "Now, here is Godfather Drosselmeier's nephew, come all the way from Nuremberg. Please behave yourself."

Marie looked up. Her godfather had on his yellow coat and his glass wig, and was smiling with pleasure. He was holding the hand of a small but very handsome young gentleman. The boy's face was hued in red and white. He wore an elegant red coat trimmed in gold, with white silk stockings and shoes, and a lovely bouquet of flowers in his shirt frill. His hair was elaborately styled and powdered, and a magnificent pigtail hung down his back. The sword at his side sparkled and shone—it seemed to be made entirely of jewels—and the hat under his arm was woven of silk.

The young man had very courtly manners. He had brought, as presents for Marie, a number of delightful toys—including the very same sugar-figures the Mouse King had destroyed. He also was carrying a beautiful saber for Fritz.

At the table he cracked nuts for everybody. Even the very hardest nut had to yield to him. He placed them in his mouth with his left hand, tugged at his pigtail with his right, and *crack!*—they all fell in pieces.

Marie grew red as a rose while she watched this charming young gentleman. She grew even redder when, after dinner, young Drosselmeier asked her to go with him to the glass cabinet in the sitting-room.

"Play together nicely, children," said Godfather Drosselmeier. "Now that my clocks are all fixed, I don't mind you playing in there."

As soon as young Drosselmeier was alone with Marie, he went down on one knee and spoke as follows: "Ah, my superb Mademoiselle Stahlbaum! See here, at your feet, the fortunate Drosselmeier whose life you saved on this very spot. You were kind enough to say that *you* would not have despised me as Princess Pirlipat did, if I had been turned ugly for your sake. When I heard your words, I immediately ceased to be a lowly Nutcracker and was restored to my former pleasing face and figure. Most exquisite lady, please bless me with your hand. Share with me my crown and kingdom, and reign with me in Marzipan Castle, for there I am now king."

Marie raised him to his feet and said gently, "Dear Mr. Drosselmeier, you are a gentle, sweet man. And you reign over a delightful country of charming and elegant people. I *will* be your bride."

So it was that Marie became young Drosselmeier's bride-to-be. In a year's time, I am told, he came to take her away in a golden coach drawn by silver horses. At the wedding, two-and-twenty thousand of the most lovely dolls danced together, all glittering with pearls and diamonds. To this day, Marie is the queen of the realm of sparkling Christmas Forests and glowing Marzipan Castles~a realm, in short, where the most wonderful things of every kind may be seen by those who have eyes to see them.

Thus ends the tale of Nutcracker and the Mouse King.

Illustrations copyright © 1996 by Roberto Innocenti

Creative Editions is an imprint of The Creative Company,
123 South Broad Street, Mankato, Minnesota 56001.

Library of Congress Cataloging-in-Publication Data

Hoffmann, E. T. A. (Ernest Theodor Amadeus), 1776–1822.
[Nussknacker und Mausekönig.   English]
Nutcracker/by E. T. A. Hoffmann; illustrated by Roberto Innocenti.
"Creative Editions."
Summary: After hearing how her toy nutcracker got his ugly face, a
small girl helps break the spell and changes him into a handsome prince.
ISBN 0-15-100227-4
[1. Fairy tales.]   I. Innocenti, Roberto, ill.   II. Title.
PZ8.H675Nt   1996 [Fic]–dc20   95–43873

First Creative Editions/Harcourt Brace edition 1996

A   B   C   D   E

Color separations by Fotoriproduzioni Grafiche, Verona
Printed in Italy by Editoriale Libraria, Trieste

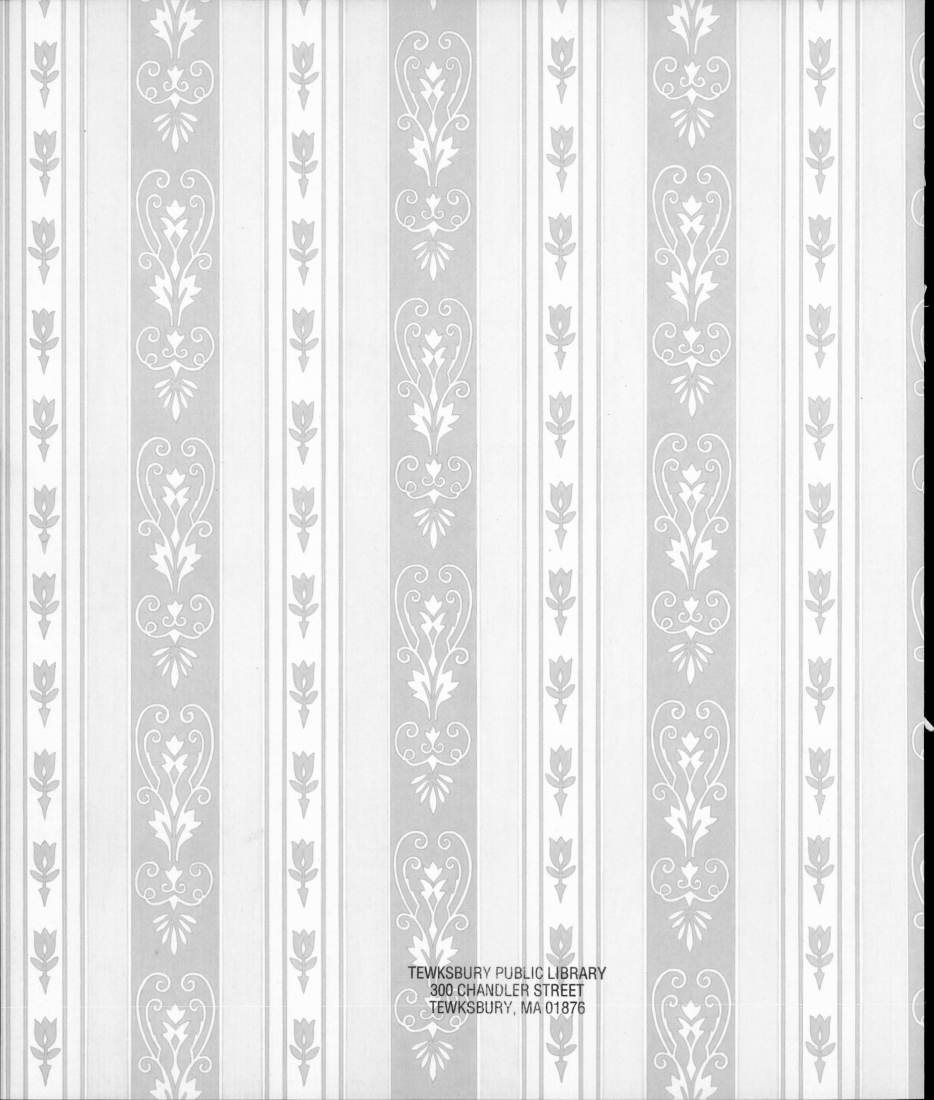